Still staring at her,
Griffin felt as if someone had
tied his tongue into a slip-knot.

She'd been beautiful before in a simple,
uncomplicated way.

Now, whatever she'd done to herself had merely
improved her features to the point of...*breathtaking.*
That was the only word he could think of. He
simply couldn't take his eyes off her.

And that mouth of hers. It seemed to be beckoning
him, as if silently whispering, *"Taste me, taste me."*

"Maggy." Her name came out half plea, half prayer,
and he mightily feared he was losing his mind. She
was stealing his senses with every touch, every
breath and he didn't seem able to stop or prevent it.

"You look...beautiful," he finally admitted with
a smile, laying his hand on her cheek. "Absolutely
beautiful."

Dear Reader,

From a Texas sweetheart to a Chicago advice columnist, our heroines will sweep you along on their journeys to happily ever after. Don't miss the tender excitement of Silhouette Romance's modern-day fairy tales!

In *Carolina's Gone A' Courting* (SR #1734), Carolina Brubaker is on a crash course with destiny—and the man of her dreams—*if* she can survive their summer of forced togetherness! Will she lasso the heart of her ambitious rancher? Find out in the next story in Carolyn Zane's THE BRUBAKER BRIDES miniseries.

To this once-burned plain Jane a worldly, sophisticated, handsome lawyer is *not* the kind of man she wants…but her heart has other plans. Be there for the transformation of this no-nonsense woman into the beauty she was meant to be, in *My Fair Maggy* (SR #1735) by Sharon De Vita.

Catch the next installment of Cathie Linz's miniseries MEN OF HONOR, *The Marine Meets His Match* (SR #1736). His favorite independent lady has agreed to play fiancée for this military man who can't resist telling her what to do. If only he could order her to *really* fall in love.…

Karen Rose Smith brings us another emotional tale of love and family with *Once Upon a Baby…* (SR #1737). This love-leery sheriff knows he should stay far away from his pretty and pregnant neighbor—he's not the husband and father type. But delivering her baby changes everything.…

I hope you enjoy every page of this month's heartwarming lineup!

Mavis C. Allen
Associate Senior Editor

Please address questions and book requests to:
Silhouette Reader Service
U.S.: 3010 Walden Ave., P.O. Box 1325, Buffalo, NY 14269
Canadian: P.O. Box 609, Fort Erie, Ont. L2A 5X3

My Fair Maggy

SHARON DE VITA

SILHOUETTE **Romance**®

Published by Silhouette Books

America's Publisher of Contemporary Romance

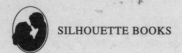 SILHOUETTE BOOKS

ISBN 0-373-19735-7

MY FAIR MAGGY

Visit Silhouette Books at www.eHarlequin.com

Printed in U.S.A.

Books by Sharon De Vita

Silhouette Romance

Heavenly Match #475
Lady and the Legend #498
Kane and Mabel #545
Baby Makes Three #573
Sherlock's Home #593
Italian Knights #610
Sweet Adeline #693
**On Baby Patrol #1276
***Baby with a Badge* #1298
***Baby and the Officer* #1316
†*The Marriage Badge* #1443
††*Anything for Her Family* #1580
††*A Family To Be* #1586
My Fair Maggy #1735

Silhouette Special Edition

Child of Midnight #1013
*The Lone Ranger #1078
**The Lady and the Sheriff* #1103
**All It Takes Is Family* #1126
†*The Marriage Basket* #1307
†*The Marriage Promise* #1313
††*With Family in Mind* #1450
††*A Family To Come Home To* #1468
Daddy Patrol #1584

Silhouette Books

The Coltons
I Married a Sheik

***Lullabies and Love
†The Blackwell Brothers
††Saddle Falls
*Silver Creek County

SHARON DE VITA,

a former adjunct professor of literature and communications, is a *USA TODAY* bestselling, award-winning author of numerous works of fiction and nonfiction. Her first novel won a national writing competition for Best Unpublished Romance Novel of 1985. This award-winning book, *Heavenly Match*, was subsequently published by Silhouette in 1985. In 1987, Sharon was the proud recipient of the *Romantic Times* Lifetime Achievement Award for Excellence in Writing.

A newlywed, Sharon met her husband while doing research for one of her books. The widowed, recently retired military officer was so wonderful, Sharon decided to marry him after she interviewed him! Sharon and her new husband have four grown children, five grandchildren, and currently reside in the Southwest.

Dear Aunt Millie,

I think I've found my Prince Charming, but I'm just a simple girl from the wrong part of town and he's a wealthy, sophisticated man who knows all the right people. Do you think there's hope that my prince might fall for me? And that I could fit into his world? I'm worried I'll embarrass myself and him at one of his fancy parties.

Cinderella in Chicago

Dear Cinderella,

Take some advice from your fairy godmother: Money and clothes do not make a man, and what really counts is what's in his heart. And yours. Be yourself and don't let wealth and artificial manners intimidate you. You might find your prince is not as interested in those "right people" and parties as much as he is interested in you and the love you have to share.

Best of luck,
Aunt Millie

Prologue

Dear Aunt Millie:

Our only son has married a lovely young woman with two small children. While we adore our new daughter-in-law, she doesn't believe in disciplining her children. During their last visit, her children flooded our bathroom, spewed four-letter words, scribbled on our walls with indelible marker, started a fire in the basement because they were smoking—they're eight and nine!—and bit our little Sheltie puppy. And this was just the first day! My son has just announced he and his wife are planning a three-week visit this summer, and I'm at my wit's end. We love our son and his family and don't want them to feel unwelcome, but I'm not certain my husband and I can survive three long weeks with these children. What should we do?

Frantic in Philly

Dear Frantic in Philly:

A hotel room is a lot cheaper than a hospital room, which is where you and your husband are headed if you put up with these monstrous children. Tell your son and his family they are more than welcome to visit. Then make a reservation for them at a nearby hotel!

Best of luck,
Aunt Millie

Chapter One

Kneeling in her garden, in a patch of warm, late-August afternoon sunlight, Maggy Gallagher didn't bother to glance up when she heard the backyard gate squeak open then squeak shut again.

But the heavy footsteps did cause her pause. Neighbors in this close-knit Chicago neighborhood were always cutting through her backyard to see either her grandfather or one of the other elderly residents who lived in the apartments above her grandfather's deli.

But her ears perked up when she heard footsteps heading toward her.

Yet she continued repotting her oregano plant, letting the cool, rich dirt slide between her fingers, humming softly until the toes of a pair of elegant black imported Italian loafers came into her line of vision.

She frowned at the toes of those shoes, a bit taken aback. Those shoes probably cost more than the entire contents of her spartan wardrobe, to say nothing of the fact that they certainly didn't belong in *this* neighborhood.

This was a hard-hat and dusty work boots kind of neighborhood. A typical working man's neighborhood.

"Mary Margaret Gallagher?" The voice that belonged to the incredibly elegant shoes was very deep, cultured, educated and…annoying. He sounded as if he was attending some formal afternoon tea instead of standing in the sweltering heat in her backyard.

Definitely Ivy League, she thought, immediately feeling self-conscious and defensive and not really knowing why. It was the kind of voice that made you want to sit up straighter, stand taller and pray you didn't have anything trailing off the heel of your shoe.

"Maggy," she corrected. From this angle, the sun was right in her eyes, so she couldn't see very much of him. Except that he was tall.

His long legs, encased in the bottom half of a very elegant, probably custom-made gray pinstripe suit, were definitely out of place in this neighborhood. The only person who ever wore a suit was Mr. Murphy, the undertaker around the corner.

"But you *are* Mary Margaret Gallagher?" he persisted, sounding a tad annoyed.

"Only to my family," she admitted, shading her eyes and tipping her head back a bit to try to get a better look at him.

"Your brother told me where to find you."

With a weary sigh, Maggy stuck her potting shovel into the dirt. "Which one?"

He frowned down at her. "Excuse me?"

"I have six brothers," Maggy explained. "Which one sent you?"

"Collin." He, too, blinked against the blazing sun.

"Collin," she acknowledged with a rueful shake of her head. "Some brothers send flowers," she muttered. "My brother sends me freeloaders."

"Excuse me?" The deep voice became even more annoyed.

"Nothing."

Maggy sighed. Like all of her brothers, Collin had both a very soft heart and a very short memory when it came to people, and he couldn't refuse anyone anything, especially if they needed help or had a problem.

Last year, after Collin, a fireman, had extinguished a small fire in the neighborhood vet's office, Maggy had come home from work to find the vet and his entire menagerie waiting for her. She had to admit, their apartment had been more than a bit cramped with an ark full of animals, as well as herself, her grandfather *and* the vet all inhabiting it together for two days.

Her brothers were notorious for sending her trouble. They thought because they came to her with their problems then she could handle everyone else's problems as well. And with three of her brothers Chicago cops, and the other three Chicago firemen, there was no end to the amount of trouble they encountered on any given day.

But Maggy figured it was probably just habit. As the oldest child, after her mother's death from cancer when Maggy had been almost twelve, not that long after their police officer father had been killed in the line of duty, she'd tried to become the female head of the household, and that included riding roughshod over her six younger brothers who had ranged in age from five through eleven, including the six-year-old twins. Over the years, her brothers had come to depend on her for help and advice—*especially* when they were in trouble.

With the deli to run and seven young kids under the age of twelve to raise, her widowed grandfather, who'd already retired from the Chicago police force on a full pension, had needed all the help he could get running a business and raising the Gallagher brood.

Glancing up at the elegant guy still standing in front of her, Maggy sighed, wondering what kind of mischief her brother had sent to brighten her day today.

She started to stand, surprised when the stranger extended a hand to help her up.

In spite of her own natural suspicions about the man, she took his hand, allowing him to help her up.

"Thank you," she mumbled, brushing off the back of her faded, slightly ragged overall shorts with a hand still tingling from his touch.

Looking at his elegant hands, Maggy self-consciously slid her own dirt-encased fingers into the pockets of her shorts.

Curious now, she blinked against the sun, then tipped her head back once more to try to see him more clearly. He towered over her by almost a foot, so the only thing she got a better view of was the underside of one very stubborn, masculine chin.

If she had to, she'd guess that he was as tall or taller than any of her brothers. Which put him somewhere near six-four or -five.

And in spite of her annoyance, she'd also have to admit that he was attractive in a blatant, arrogant-male sort of way.

Rich black hair framed a face tanned to perfection, emphasizing enormous blue eyes that bordered on silver. Like a wolf's, Maggy thought absently, feeling a quick shiver slither over her. And a very wary, suspicious wolf at that.

His face comprised sharp planes and angles, and if she

wasn't mistaken, those were worry lines in his forehead. She knew because her brothers had given her more than a few in her lifetime.

Styled hair. Fancy suit. Self-important posture.

Definitely trouble, she decided. And definitely the kind of man to set her nerves on edge.

Just like her ex-husband.

She almost shuddered at the thought of Dennis. They'd met his last year in college; he'd been prelaw, she'd been a twenty-year-old sophomore stunned and surprised that someone like him—gorgeous, elegant and sophisticated, not to mention from a wealthy, prominent East Coast family—would even notice her.

But he had, and when he'd asked her to marry him right after his graduation, before leaving for Notre Dame law school, she'd readily agreed, dropping out of college to follow him to Indiana.

His well-to-do parents had been horrified by their marriage and told Dennis he was on his own financially. Instead of returning to school to finish *her* education, she'd taken a full-time job to support them so that Dennis could continue his.

Within three months of his law-school graduation—with honors—he'd announced that he was returning to his family's estate on Long Island, New York, and quite frankly, she no longer "fit" into his life. He went on to tell her that she had no education, hadn't really grown with him, and quite honestly was simply too unsophisticated to fit into the world he intended to move in. And then, of course, there was the embarrassment of her family.

She probably could have done without such honesty.

Devastated and heartbroken at his callousness and her own naiveté, and infuriated that he believed her beloved, large Irish family beneath him, she'd come home to her grandfather, vowing never again to risk her heart for love or a man.

She should have listened to her inner voice when it warned her that she and Dennis had been far too different and from two different worlds ever to find happiness, but she'd been in love, and at the time had believed love conquered all.

Now older and wiser, she knew better.

And knew enough to recognize another man like her ex-husband was standing in front of her. He was one of those men who was brimming with good looks and confidence, a confidence borne of the elemental understanding that they would always belong in the world they moved in.

In the same way she had come to understand—painfully so—that it was a world she would *never* belong in.

It didn't matter, Maggy told herself. Not any longer. She knew who she was, and more important, who she *wasn't*. And she'd long ago stopped trying to impress guys like him.

"So, what can I do for you?" she asked.

"My name is Griffin J. Gibson the Third."

She fought the urge to laugh. So he had a mouthful of a name to go with the fancy suit.

"The third?" she repeated with a lift of her eyebrow, unable to stop a smile. Clearly this was a man who was quite impressed with his own importance. It amused her to no end.

"Yes, the third," Griffin repeated in a tone that probably left his staff of underlings quivering but didn't impress her at all.

"And, uh…what does the J stand for?" she asked, desperately trying not to show her amusement.

"Jedediah," he said coolly.

"Figures," she muttered with a shake of her head and a smile.

Griffin's jaw tensed and his eyes narrowed. For some reason, he had the unmistakable feeling this adorable little dirt urchin was making fun of him. And it was annoying the hell out of him.

Admittedly, she was unmistakably gorgeous with a riotous cap of short strawberry-blond curls, a pert, upturned nose dotted with myriad freckles and a luxuriously full unpainted mouth.

She might have the innocent dewy looks of a saint, he decided, but she definitely had the mouth of a sinner.

He also had to admit she had a natural beauty that surprised him. Perhaps he'd grown so accustomed to the plastic, artificial beauty of the women his father kept marrying, that he'd forgotten there were woman in the world who were beautiful without any artifice.

She wasn't tall, in fact she barely reached his chin, and that was probably a stretch, but he had to admit she was one fetching feminine package.

Although he usually preferred cool, calm society women who didn't demand any kind of emotional or marital commitment, he found himself more than a little intrigued by the bundle of unlikely femininity standing in front of him.

Maybe it was just a knee-jerk reaction to his recent breakup with Marissa. Who would have guessed that cool, classy Marissa would suddenly expect—no—*demand* a commitment from him?

They had dated for almost a year, a totally casual noncommittal relationship. They'd been upfront with each other from day one: neither was interested in any kind of permanency or emotional commitment—simply a casual relationship.

So he was totally bewildered and stunned two months ago when Marissa announced she thought it was time for their relationship to move on to the next step: a very public engagement followed by a lavish Chicago society wedding.

He felt tricked and deemed her behavior blatantly unfair.

And unfortunately, he'd felt it necessary to tell her so.

She hadn't taken it well, he remembered, calling him several unrepeatable names, and then as the final insult, she'd accused him of being *worse* than his father.

That had almost caused him to lose his infamous self-control along with his temper.

He was nothing like his father. *Nothing.* While his father may have been a successful businessman, he was a dismal failure in personal matters. The man had married and divorced seven women in the last twenty-five years. Each woman had grown younger and younger and more interested in his bankroll than in his heart.

For the life of him, Griffin simply could not understand how such a brilliant businessman could continually be outwitted by half-witted females. His father's behavior was, if nothing else, an embarrassment.

Which was why Griffin was determined never to let any woman make a fool of him. He'd learned the hard way that they were fickle and deceitful, and certainly not to be trusted.

In his experience with Marissa, as well as with watching his father over the years, he'd learned firsthand that women said one thing but generally wanted something else.

It was a sly sort of subterfuge, using pretty words and

pretty faces to disguise their usually devious ulterior motives. As he'd learned once again with Marissa, a woman would say anything to get what she wanted, while truth generally had no bearing. This most recent female experience had simply reinforced what he'd learned and believed for so long about the true nature of women's motives. And he was not about to ever let a woman make a laughingstock of him the way so many had his father.

He was far too prideful for that. So perhaps that's why he was so surprised by his reaction to the woman standing before him.

Letting his gaze roam over her again, from the top of her head to the toes of her threadbare sneakers, stopping at various points of interest in between, he realized that he was having a very unusual reaction, unlike any he'd ever had before.

It simply puzzled him. Truly. He never responded to women in this manner.

"Are you finished?" Maggy snapped, planting one hand on her slender hip.

"Finished?" He felt confused for a moment. Her scent had distracted him, and he was a man who was never distracted. Especially by a female. She smelled of fresh dirt, sunshine and, if he wasn't mistaken, vanilla. An incredibly interesting combination of scents, he decided.

"Are you finished inspecting me?" He wasn't the first male to give her the once-over, and probably wouldn't be the last. But she didn't particularly care for the way he looked at her. It could only be described as deliberate male interest. The kind of interest that acknowledged without a word that he was a male and she was a female. It made her feel as if he'd just peeled away her clothes and left her standing in the hot sun in nothing but her birthday suit.

Something about the way those eyes raked her made her body feel warm and flushed all over. As if she was running a fever. It annoyed her to no end that a man who just looked so wrong for her could cause her heart to pound and her palms to dampen.

What on earth was wrong with her instincts? Had they gone haywire somewhere along the line?

Or had she forgotten the hard-earned lessons of her ex-husband who'd made it clear that men like him didn't want, need or respect women like her? She simply didn't fit in their *lifestyle.* Even now, several years after their dismal divorce, the term still grated on her nerves.

Maggy glared at Griffin, a man so like her ex-husband, and realized she was totally unnerved by his visual appraisal and annoyed by his audacity.

Lifting a finger, Griffin rubbed his eyebrow, trying to suppress a smile. "Well, Mary Margaret, I can't say your brother didn't warn me."

Griffin let the smile loose. Used to the logical grid of Chicago's downtown and the Gold Coast, he'd gotten lost in the maze of one-way streets in this old, ethnic neighborhood and had stopped at the local fire station to get directions. He'd been surprised when Maggy's brother Collin had stepped forward, not only offering directions but also offering some advice for dealing with his sister. Much to Griffin's surprise, Collin had told him that if he was going to see Maggy, he'd better mind his step. She was…a pistol. Something Griffin was learning for himself.

"Warn you about what?" she demanded suspiciously, cocking her head to study him with the same intensity he'd studied her.

"About your temper and your temperament."

Planting her hands on her hips, Maggy huffed out a breath, obviously trying to hold on to her composure. "I don't have a temper and my temperament is just fine, thank you."

"Yes, I can see that, Mary Margaret," Griffin said, his grin sliding wider as he slipped both hands back into his pockets again.

"Don't call me Mary Margaret," she snapped crossly.

"But it's your name, isn't it?" he asked mildly, totally and thoroughly amused now. So much emotion, he thought, wondering if she'd also have that kind of passion. It was, he decided, quite an interesting thought.

"That's entirely beside the point. As I told you, only my family calls me by my given name. If Collin sent you, you must be in some kind of trouble."

He started to explain Collin hadn't sent him, but had merely given him correct directions, but she held up her hand, stopping him.

"I can put you to work in the deli for a few days so you can earn some money. And there's a small, empty apartment in the basement of my building if you need a place to stay, but no drinking. No drugs. And definitely no women."

"You run a tight ship," he commented casually, rocking back on his heels.

"Exactly. And if you break the rules, you're out. Do you understand?"

"Perfectly," he said, not bothering to hide his amusement. "Now tell me, Mary Margaret, do I look like the kind of man who needs a job and a place to stay?" The mere idea was so ludicrous he couldn't possibly be offended.

There was humor in his voice and in his eyes, and yet Maggy didn't know why she didn't find the situation or him at all amusing. The man simply made her...nervous. Cautious. On guard.

She blew out a sigh of frustration. "Looks can be deceiving. Trouble comes calling regardless of money or position." Maggy hesitated a moment. "Besides, I learned a long time ago never to judge anyone by their clothing or their appearance."

"Sounds like a sound practice," he agreed.

"Besides, Collin wouldn't have sent you to me unless you needed something or were in some kind of trouble."

"An expert at handling trouble, are you?" he asked with a lift of his eyebrow.

"I'm a regular Aunt Millie," she snapped referring to the famous advice columnist.

"So I've heard," he said simply, causing her eyes to narrow suspiciously.

"What are you talking about?" Maggy frowned as a warning bell began to clang in her head. "What have you heard? Have my brothers been telling tall tales about me again?" She wanted to roll her eyes. Practical jokes had been a long-standing Gallagher tradition for as far back as she could remember. Each of her brothers tried to outdo the other. And more times then not, she was the butt of all those jokes.

"Since you asked, there is something I need."

"If it's not a place to stay or a job, then what?" she asked nervously.

"I want you to accompany me to my grandmother's house for lunch tomorrow."

She frowned at him. "You got all dressed up in that monkey suit, bothered my brother Collin, simply to ask me to have lunch with you at your grandmother's house?"

"Well, yes and no," he said, making her frown.

Her fists clenched in frustration and she simply glared at him. "Do you think you could make up your mind here?"

"It's not that simple," he said, realizing the well-rehearsed explanation he'd put together this morning over breakfast with his grandmother had been blown to smithereens the moment he'd laid eyes on Maggy. And it was rare, very rare, for him to be thrown off his game. Personally or professionally. But something about this woman had simply thrown him totally off course.

"Do you think you could simplify it for me?" Maggy asked.

"My grandmother would like you to have lunch with her tomorrow," he said, rushing on when her eyebrows rose. "I'll be happy to accompany you and join you as well."

"You don't trust your grandmother to eat lunch on her own?" Maggy asked with another frown.

He couldn't help it, he chuckled. "Are you deliberately being difficult?" he asked, cocking his head to look at her and realizing if he kept looking at her, he was going to continue to be distracted.

"No, actually, when I'm being deliberately difficult, it's really a sight to behold," she said, grinning. "And if you don't believe me, I have six brothers who'll vouch for me."

"No, I'll take your word for it." He paused for a moment. "Let me see if we can start this over in a way that makes a bit more sense."

"Now, that would be refreshing."

"My grandmother would very much like to meet you and has asked me to extend an invitation to you to join us for lunch tomorrow. Is that a bit clearer?"

"Who's your grandmother and why on earth does she want to have lunch with me?" Maggy looked at him carefully. "I don't even know her, do I?"

She wondered if perhaps his grandmother could be someone from the neighborhood, then immediately dismissed the thought. No one in the neighborhood could have a grandson who looked like this without everyone knowing about it.

"Everyone knows my grandmother." He smiled at her. "My grandmother is Aunt Millie."

For a moment, Maggy merely stared at him as recognition clicked in her mind. Maggy had to swallow. Hard. "Your grandmother is Aunt Millie? The newspaper's Aunt Millie? The advice columnist?"

He merely grinned. "Yes, my grandmother is all of the above."

"Why?" she asked, looking at him carefully. "Why on earth does your grandmother want to meet *me?* I mean, how on earth does she even know me or about me?" A sudden thought had Maggy's nerves calming. "This is a joke, right? Collin or one of my other brothers put you up to this." She laughed. "I should have known. They're forever playing practical jokes on everyone, but I'm not about to fall for this one. It was a nice try, though," she added, reaching out to pat his cheek in a patronizing way.

Griffin stiffened at her touch, wondering why his cheek was tingling, and why he felt a rush of heat where her fingers had met his skin. "I can assure you, Mary Margaret, this is not a joke." He looked at her carefully. "No one put me up to this nor do I engage in practical jokes."

"Now, why doesn't that surprise me?" she said.

Griffin's jaw tightened. "Trust me, I don't joke about business matters, nor matters concerning my grandmother." Because she was still looking at him as if she expected him to shout "gotcha" at any moment, Griffin raised his hand in the air. "Honest."

Half the business leaders in the nation considered his mere word his bond, but here he was, standing in the middle of a dirt yard raising his hand as if taking an oath like a misbehaved five-year-old.

But he had no pride when it came to his grandmother because quite simply he adored her.

His grandmother had been the one, loving, stable influence in his life. She and his grandfather—until his death two years ago—had raised and nurtured him, giving him a sense of stability and security as well as their own high sense of morals and ethics that had been the foundation of his life.

And he'd not stand by and let anyone hurt his grandmother. Not while there was a breath left in his body.

"Maybe this might explain things a bit better." Growing a little frustrated himself, he reached in his pocket and extracted an envelope, handing it to her.

"What's this?"

"Read it, I think it might explain everything."

"Fine, I'll read it." Maggy glanced down at the envelope, which was addressed to Mrs. Millicent Gibson at some fancy Lake Shore Drive address with the return address of the deli on the front.

"This is my grandfather's handwriting," she said in surprise, slipping out the folded letter and reading carefully. "Oh no," she muttered, trying hard not to grind her teeth in absolute, total frustration. "He didn't," she said, eyes widening as she glanced up at Griffin in mortification. "I can't believe it." Stunned, Maggy shook her head. "I simply can't believe he did something like this. Again."

Chapter Two

"I'm going to strangle my grandfather when I get my hands on him," Maggy seethed, grinding her teeth in spite of her resolve and feeling mortally embarrassed.

"Are you telling me you didn't know about this?" Griffin asked in genuine surprise.

"Know about it?" Maggy shook her head, wishing the ground would open up and swallow her whole. "I didn't have a clue." Maggy's eyes slid closed and she tried to rein in her dwindling composure. "I'm sorry, but this is all a mistake. A big, huge mistake."

Glancing at Griffin J. Gibson III, Maggy blew out a weary breath. "I'm terribly, terribly sorry," she said, meaning it. "I have no idea why my grandfather wrote all that stuff about me to your grandmother," she admitted, flushing when she recalled her grandfather's words.

"So you're not inquisitive and intelligent with a strong dose of common sense and fair play? Not to mention that you possess a great deal of wisdom and faith?" he asked with a smile.

"No—yes. I—" Frustrated, Maggy shook her head. "He makes me sound like Solomon," she all but cried.

"Well, if it's any consolation, Mary Margaret, you certainly don't look like Solomon."

"This isn't funny," she moaned, shaking her head. "How my grandfather could have written to your grandmother without even consulting me and suggested that I'd be perfect to take over her advice column now that she's retiring is simply beyond my comprehension."

What on earth had her grandfather been thinking? She was in no position to be giving advice to anyone, especially about what to do with his or her life considering the mess she'd made of her own. She hadn't even managed to stay married five years, for Pete's sake! So how on earth did her grandfather expect her to give others advice about their lives?

"So you really didn't know about this?" Griffin asked.

"Of course not," Maggy snapped. "You can't honestly think I knew about, or approved of it?" She all but glared at him, insulted that he apparently doubted her word.

"I don't know what to believe," he admitted with a shake of his head.

Griffin looked at her again. Carefully. She was not at all what he'd expected, granted, but then again he wasn't quite certain what to expect. Although someone a bit more…sophisticated was more what he'd had in mind.

He simply couldn't believe that her grandfather—an old beau of his grandmother's—just *happened* to begin writing to his grandmother after nearly forty years of silence suggesting he had the perfect person to take over his grandmother's column, his grandmother's very lucrative column. Even to Griffin's cynical mind, the idea had seemed more than a bit far-fetched. And made him inherently suspicious of both of them and their motives.

From the moment of the public announcement that his grandmother was retiring and the nationwide search to find a replacement to take over her advice column, he'd been deluged with résumés from professionals with Ph.D.'s in psychology, marital counseling and social work as well as master's degrees in business, law and humanities, to say nothing of the reams of résumés from lawyers, doctors, judges and psychiatrists and just about anyone else with some kind of advanced degree or education who believed they were qualified to take over his grandmother's column.

To think that an uneducated deli waitress who lived in a run-down neighborhood and who probably hadn't ever been outside her own little world in her entire lifetime was qualified, let alone suitable, to take over his grandmother's column was simply ludicrous.

His grandmother might be inclined to consider this woman as her replacement simply out of some misguided feeling of goodwill for past ties with her grandfather, but he had no past ties to these people, nor any goodwill. And his cynical, suspicious mind found the whole thing just a tad bit contrived, not to mention convenient.

If he hadn't learned to be both cynical and suspicious watching his father bed and wed one beautiful young gold digger after the other over the past twenty-five years, he certainly would have learned in law school and the succeeding ten years he'd spent as head of not only his grandmother's business affairs but also his own law firm.

"Maggy girl," her grandfather called from the back porch of their third-floor apartment, making Maggy groan. "Who's that handsome young lad out there with you?" Her grandfather grinned down at them.

"Grandpa." Maggy fisted her hands at her sides and glared up at her beloved grandfather, shaking the letter at him. "I want to talk to you."

"Aye, well then," Patrick Gallagher muttered, sensing trouble as he eyed the man with his granddaughter. If his old eyes weren't deceiving him, this was Millicent's handsome young grandson. Pleasure stole through Patrick, and in spite of a bad hip, he felt like dancing an Irish jig of joy. He and Millicent had been certain there'd be romantic sparks between their grandchildren—if only they could have a chance to meet, which he'd decided to help along. He grinned down at them now, thrilled that apparently their plan was working.

Uh-oh. Patrick's eyebrows drew together when he got a good look at their faces and saw the tension simmering between them. Even from up here it was hard to miss. He wanted to sigh in frustration, but then he brightened. Aye, it wasn't all bad, he decided. A bit of spirit never hurt a romance none. In fact, a bit of it merely added to the heat and fire, binding a couple together like nothing else.

Delighted, Patrick glanced down at the couple again, knowing he was going to have to slip out of the house, if the look on his granddaughter's face was any sign of her mood. Aye, he adored his only granddaughter—his Maggy was one in a million—but he sorely wished she wasn't quite so…high-spirited. She reminded him of her late grandmother, who'd had quite a bit of spirit of her own, he remembered fondly.

"Come on up then, Maggy girl," he called, already planning his escape. "And bring that handsome young lad with you." Cursing his bad hip and the cane that slowed his movements, Patrick slipped inside the house, snatched his forbidden pipe from his hidey-hole in the dining room, then headed directly toward the front stairs where he could slip out unnoticed before Maggy and the lad got in the door.

"Your grandfather, I presume?" Griffin asked. He glanced at Maggy again, feeling an uncomfortable tightening in his gut. Could her grandfather be on the level? Could he really have just believed that his granddaughter might be his grandmother's heir apparent?

What on earth was the old man thinking? Griffin wondered. Perhaps he was suffering from some type of mental malady that impaired his judgment. That would certainly explain all of this.

On the other hand, if he wasn't, there were more than enough reasons—monetary reasons—for Griffin to be suspicious. The income from his grandmother's column was more than enough money to share—and much more than any deli income could provide, more than enough to make someone want to try to play on his grandmother's kind heart and sympathies in order to charm his way into her good graces merely to have a crack at those very lucrative contracts.

Seeing the suspicion on his face, Maggy felt her temper simmer. "Look, pal, I don't know who you think you are, or what you think you're implying, but you're beginning to annoy me," Maggy warned.

"I'm *just* beginning to annoy you? Well, I can't wait to see how you act when you're fully engaged and annoyed."

"I think I'd better talk to my grandfather," Maggy said, trying hard not to grit her teeth. "Now."

With a nod, Griffin followed her across the yard, up two flights of rickety stairs, feeling a bout of sympathy for her grandfather. From the fire in the woman's eyes, he had a feeling what was about to transpire was not going to be pleasant.

"Grandpa," Maggy called as she slammed in the back door. "Grandpa, where are you?"

Silence greeted her. "Matchmaking is one thing. Setting up blind dates for me is another. But this…this…ooh!" Maggy stepped deeper into the empty kitchen. "Grandpa!"

Griffin cleared his throat, wondering if she even remembered he was there. "I…uh…take it he's disappeared," he said with a glance around the empty kitchen, trying not to be amused.

"He's no dummy," Maggy muttered, still clutching the blasted letter in her fist. "He had to know that eventually you'd show up here." She turned to him again, shaking her head. "And I'm sorry you've wasted a trip as well as your time."

A momentary bout of panic set in. Griffin might adore his grandmother, but she had a will as stubborn as steel, and if he didn't set up a luncheon appointment so his grandmother could at least meet Maggy Gallagher and get a chance to appease herself and her curiosity about this woman, and see for herself how ludicrous the whole idea was, she would never give up this silly idea of considering Maggy to take over her column.

"Maggy," he said carefully. "From what I've gathered, this is something your grandfather came up with on his own, correct?"

"More than correct," she snapped, wondering if she should start searching under the beds for her grandfather.

"Well, if he's as stubborn as my grandmother, this is obviously something they've cooked up together."

She turned to him slowly, then frowned as the thought registered. "What do you mean?" Maggy shook her head. "I don't even think my grandfather knows your grandmother."

Griffin sighed. "Apparently they've been acquainted for many years."

"My grandfather knows Aunt Millie?" she said, her voice edging upward in shock.

"Yes," Griffin admitted with a smile. "Apparently before my grandfather, *your* grandfather was her paramour." Griffin banked a smile. "According to my grandmother they were quite an item." Even he had a hard time believing his elegant, sophisticated grandmother had been involved with this neighborhood deli owner. It was, quite frankly, ludicrous as far as he was concerned.

"Paramour?" Maggy blinked at him, trying to get this idea straight in her mind. It was a mistake to look directly at him, Maggy realized. He was far too gorgeous. Her pulse began to thrum wildly, and she absently pressed the heel of her hand to her heart where the beat had sped up as well. "An item?" Still reeling from his words and her own reaction to Griffin, Maggy dully shook her head, trying to take it all in. She had a hard time believing her grandfather had been an item or a paramour with anyone but her late grandmother. And if he had, he'd never mentioned it to Maggy.

"Yes, and apparently they've been corresponding since my grandfather's death several years ago." His gaze remained steady on her face, watching myriad emotions flit across her features, darken her eyes, tighten her mouth. And a luscious mouth it was, feeling a tightening in his gut. For an instant, a fraction of an instant, he wondered what she'd taste like. If she'd taste as sweet as she looked.

"Corresponding," she repeated dully.

"Yes, and if I know my grandmother she's not going to give up until she at least meets you."

"Meets me?" Maggy almost shuddered. The idea of

meeting Aunt Millie was enough to scare her out of her shoes. Aunt Millie wasn't just a nationally recognized advice columnist, she was the doyenne of Chicago's social elite. Right up there in the same category with Maggy's former in-laws.

She'd rather have a root canal than meet or begin associating with anyone like that—or someone like *this man* again. He was Dennis all over again, she realized dully, letting her gaze go over Griffin once more.

Granted, he was far more polished, and a great deal more handsome than Dennis, not to mention polite and appealing, but the facade couldn't change who and what he was. Or who his grandmother was, and Maggy wasn't about to get involved with people like this ever again. Once burned, twice shy. Although Maggy wasn't certain *shy* was a word anyone would ever use to describe her.

Fear and annoyance stiffened her resolve.

"Mr. Griffin," she said coldly. "Trust me, in spite of my grandfather's shenanigans, I have no intention or interest in taking over your grandmother's column. I'm sure it's a very nice column, but trust me it's not on my list of things to do, nor do I have any qualifications for such a job. So please thank your grandmother for her kindness and consideration as well as the luncheon invitation, but there's really no point in our meeting."

Her grandfather must have been sipping the Irish whiskey again before he wrote that letter, she thought, glancing around the empty, quiet kitchen and wondering just where he'd disappeared to now.

It didn't matter. At the moment all that mattered was getting rid of Griffin J. Gibson III. The man made her far too nervous for her own peace of mind.

Rudeness be damned, she walked to the open back door

and opened it farther, clearly inviting him to leave. "My grandfather apparently has had a severe lapse in judgment, not to mention a severe lapse in memory, since he promised me less than two months ago that he'd never interfere in my personal life. Again," she added with a heavy sigh. "So I'm afraid you've wasted your time. And a trip," she added.

"Maggy," Griffin said. "Have dinner with me?"

The mere thought of spending more time with this man, alone, was enough to make her break out in hives.

"I'm not hungry," she snapped. "And it's a little early for dinner," she added with a lift of her eyebrow, glancing at the large clock on the wall in the kitchen. "It's barely noon."

He smiled, slipping a hand in his pocket, realizing this woman was going to be a challenge, something he hadn't encountered in quite a long time. At least not where a woman was concerned. For some reason the idea amused and intrigued him. She was quite fascinating, he decided. Rude, a bit rough around the edges, but more fascinating than any woman he'd met in a very long time.

"Not now," he corrected with a chuckle, admiring her forthrightness. In his experience, it was a rare commodity where women were concerned. "Tonight." Cocking his head, he studied her, once again feeling that intense pull deep in his gut and trying to ignore it to concentrate on the problem at hand. "Apparently our grandparents have cooked up some kind of plan here, and unless we do something to appease them, I have a feeling neither of them is going to let this rest."

"Or let us be," Maggy finished for him with a moan, realizing he had a point.

"Exactly," he concurred. "I don't know about your grandfather, but my grandmother is as stubborn as the day is long."

"My grandfather has her beat hands down," Maggy admitted with a frown. "He gets an idea in his head and doesn't give up until he gets his own way."

"That's what I thought," Griffin murmured. "So unless you and I join forces, have dinner to discuss this situation and come up with some kind of plan of our own to foil whatever they have in mind, I have a feeling our lives are about to get complicated." Griffin sighed. "Very complicated." He glanced at his watch, not wanting to give her time to think up another excuse. "Shall we say seven at the Plantation downtown?"

"Seven?" she repeated, her mind still reeling.

"Yes." He started toward the door, wanting to get out while the getting was good. "Do you know where the Plantation is located? I can send a car for you if you like."

"A car?" Maggy shook her head, her eyes locked on his. "No," she whispered, licking her lips and wondering what on earth was wrong with her voice. He'd stopped right in front of her, standing close enough for her to feel his body heat. Maggy refused to step back, refused to back down, and refused to acknowledge the effect he was having on her. "No, that won't be necessary," she said with a bit more force. "I'll take a cab. Thank you."

"Fine, I'll see you tonight." He simply stood there, his gaze locked on hers, electricity humming and simmering between them like a live wire let loose. "Thanks, Maggy. I appreciate it." Unable to resist, and knowing he simply had to touch her before he left, Griffin lifted a hand, running a finger down her nose to remove a smudge of dirt.

Maggy's eyes widened and she all but reared back like a startled foe. He smiled, wondering why his finger was tingling where he'd touched her.

"You…uh…had a smudge of dirt on your nose," he said quietly.

Absently, Maggy rubbed her own nose, wondering why her body was vibrating like strings on a Stradivarius violin.

She didn't want him touching her; she didn't want herself responding to him. Nor did she want to be reminded that she was a healthy young woman, and a man like this could touch her and send her body into betrayal.

"Until tonight, then." Griffin reached for the letter she still held clutched in her hand. Their fingers brushed and he felt a jolt through his entire system. Stunned, he hesitated a moment before stepping through the door, looking at her curiously. "Goodbye, Maggy," he said, glancing back at her before descending the stairs. "Until tonight."

"Goodbye," she whispered, lifting her tingling fingers to her lips, and wondering what on earth had just happened.

Taking a deep breath, Maggy waited until he'd cleared the door before slamming it, then leaned against it, grateful he was gone.

Shaking her head to clear it, Maggy realized she wasn't quite certain what had just happened. All she knew was that it scared her—Griffin scared her because of what he made her feel, what he made her remember, and worse, because he reminded her of the things she'd always thought she wanted.

A home, a husband, a family of her own.

Now she knew how very much her wants could cost her. She'd decided the day she'd come home, after her divorce from Dennis was final, that she'd never again risk her heart or her pride for a man.

And Griffin J. Gibson III was a dangerous man, she decided. Dangerous to her heart and her peace of mind simply because of who he was and what he made her feel. And now she had to spend an entire evening with him—because of her grandfather's latest harebrained scheme.

Feeling ill at the thought, Maggy glanced at the kitchen clock again, wondering if it was too late to get out of her dinner engagement with Griffin. Probably. And he did have a point. If they didn't do something, her grandfather would never give up this wild idea.

She had less than seven hours until dinner. Seven hours to talk to her grandfather and get this mess straightened out before she met Griffin and put an end to this nonsense once and for all.

So much for a relaxing evening at home on her day off, Maggy thought with a scowl.

"Grandpa!" Maggy's voice bellowed through the empty house. One thing at a time, she decided. First she'd handle her grandfather, and then, she thought with firm resolve, she'd handle Griffin J. Gibson III. "You've really done it this time!"

The Plantation was one of the oldest, most exclusive restaurants in the city of Chicago. It was located in the heart of downtown, and reservations were made months in advance since the food, service and ambience were among the finest and most expensive in the city.

The decor was simple and elegant. Pale white silk on the walls, subdued lighting enhanced by candles flickering on every table and black leather club booths that accommodated four people comfortably, or two intimately, depending on which booth was chosen by the maître d'.

Griffin had been a regular for many years and had his own small booth reserved in the back of the restaurant where he would be guaranteed both privacy as well as anonymity. He was a man who valued both.

Griffin leaned back against the booth, sipping his wine, watching the other diners and waiters.

He knew the moment Maggy entered the small, elegant restaurant. He felt her before he saw her and, totally unnerved by the experience, picked up his wine again with hands that were far too shaky for his liking.

His gaze sought and found her, standing and smiling up at the maître d'. For some reason, he felt a pinch of jealousy nip at him and ruthlessly banked it down, telling himself he was being ridiculous.

She wore a simple black sheath dress and black high heels that made her long legs look longer and sexy as hell. The sheath was by no means tight, yet it caressed her body in a way that showed off her slender figure and feminine curves. His mouth went dry watching as she walked toward him, and he stood up, extending his hand to her.

"Maggy." He took her hand, felt its warmth and softness. She looked fresh and polished, and incredibly beautiful in her very no-frills, no-nonsense way. It stirred something deep inside him. "I'm so glad you could make it."

"You didn't give me much choice," she said, sliding into the opposite side of the booth, realizing she was practically leg to leg with him. She was certain the booth was designed for intimate dinners not practical business discussions, which she'd convinced herself this was.

He laughed. "Would you like a drink? A glass of wine perhaps?" He held up his own glass of pale gold and she nodded.

"That would be fine." She took her napkin from the table and unfolded it into her lap. She knew her hands and knees were shaking, but she was going to relax, get this over with, and then get out of here and say goodbye to this man.

She glanced up at him to find him watching her curiously. She thought she'd imagined the masculine power that radiated from him, but being so close to him once again, she realized she hadn't imagined it—it was very, very real.

And made her very self-conscious.

"So, did you ever find your grandfather?" Griffin asked as the waiter poured her a glass of wine and set it in front of her.

"Oh, I found him all right," Maggy admitted, sipping her wine and smiling in surprise. "This is wonderful," she said, taking another sip.

"Good. Good." Griffin tasted his own wine again, pleased that she liked hers. "And what did he have to say for himself?"

Maggy sighed, then glanced around so she wouldn't be forced to look at Griffin. Looking into that gorgeous face made her mind mush. "He said that he couldn't understand why I was so upset. That any egghead could see that I was the perfect person to take over Aunt Millie's column, which is why he suggested it to her." Maggy shook her head, still dumbfounded by what her grandfather considered common sense. She risked glancing up at Griffin and saw amusement twinkling in his eyes, which immediately made her defensive. "I don't think this is funny."

"No, I imagine you don't. I'm afraid I don't either, Maggy," he admitted. "But apparently our grandparents are determined about this matter, and as we agreed earlier, when they're determined, nothing stops them. So tell me, why does your grandfather think you're perfect to take over the column?"

Embarrassed, Maggy shrugged, her slender shoulders moving restlessly. "I guess just because everyone in the family—and the neighborhood—comes to me with their problems. My parents died when we were very young," she explained with another shrug. "I was the oldest and the only girl. Naturally, my six younger brothers started coming to me with their problems." Smiling in remembrance, Maggy glanced up at him, caught off guard by the intensity of his look. "It seems like every time they got into some kind of trouble, they expected me to bail them out."

"And you did?" he asked, sipping his wine, finding himself admiring the fact that she apparently was so reliable as well as responsible when it came to her family. Since he considered loyalty to family one of the most admirable traits any person could have, he found himself more and more intrigued by Maggy.

Loyalty was not usually a trait he associated with women. On the contrary, it was just the opposite, he realized, thinking about how Maggy was shattering all his long-held beliefs about them.

Maggy nodded. "Grandpa raised us after my parents' deaths, and raising seven kids under twelve wasn't easy while trying to run a deli." She offered him a smile. "He needed all the help he could get."

"I can imagine." Griffin laughed. "What I can't imagine is what it would be like having six brothers," he said, and she thought she detected a wistful note in his voice.

"Do you have any brothers?"

"No," he admitted. "I'm an only child. And my grandmother and grandfather raised me after my mother's death when I was eight." For the life of him he had no idea why he'd confided this to her. He never confided personal information to anyone.

She looked at him carefully, sensing something he wasn't saying. "What about your father, Griffin?" Maggy asked quietly, making him shift uncomfortably.

"My father," he repeated, glancing up and away from her, but not before she saw the pain, raw and real, in his eyes. "He's a brilliant attorney and businessman, but when it comes to women, I'm afraid he's a hopeless romantic with little common sense." He hesitated, then took a breath, realizing she was still looking at him expectantly, waiting for an answer. "He left us when I was seven, shortly before my mother got ill. He and his new wife—the second of his seven wives I should point out—weren't particularly interested in having a little boy cramp their style."

"Seven wives?" Maggy said, stunned. She shook her head, trying to absorb this. "Your father has been married seven times?"

He laughed but the sound held no humor, only pain and bitterness as he glanced at his watch. "Well, it might be eight by now. What day is it?" He didn't add that each of his father's wives became younger and younger as the years went on. He wasn't even certain the latest one was old enough to drink or vote.

"Oh, Griffin, I'm so sorry." Instinctively, Maggy reached across the table and covered his hand with hers, her heart aching for him and the pain he was trying so very hard to conceal. Clearly his father's abandonment had had a profound effect on him as a child, and the effects were still visible on the man. It softened her heart toward him in a way that nothing else could. Family was the heart and soul of her, everything that mattered, and the idea of someone in her own family abandoning her—the way Griffin's father had abandoned him—made pain curl through her. She couldn't even begin to imagine living with such unbearable agony.

No wonder the man was so suspicious and cynical, she realized. He couldn't help it. How could he not be? Knowing his own father hadn't wanted him, had abandoned him and his mother for some other woman—women, Maggy mentally corrected, when he was a helpless child was totally and unforgivably unconscionable.

"Don't be sorry," he said coolly, sipping his wine with his free hand. "It worked out for the best." His smile bloomed, bright and brilliant, but she knew he was desperately trying to hide the pain. "My grandparents were wonderful surrogate parents, and I had a wonderful childhood." He hesitated. "I absolutely adored my grandparents. Still do," he added with a sigh. "Which is why I'm so concerned about my grandmother and her column."

"I understand." Maggy smiled, feeling as if they'd finally found some common ground—their loyalty to their grandparents—as well as a bit of understanding as to why he was so cynical and suspicious: his love and loyalty to his grandmother. She understood that completely. "As much as my grandfather drives me and all my brothers crazy with his wild schemes and matchmaking ploys, I have to admit I adore him." Laughing, Maggy shook her head. "He means well, it's just his methods that are a bit…skewed."

"So you believe he wrote that letter to my grandmother simply because he believed you really were a good candidate to take over her column?"

Maggy narrowed her gaze on Griffin for a moment. "Why else do you think he would have written it?" she asked, feeling his suspicion as hot and heavy as a wave and trying not to let it upset her.

But this was her grandfather they were talking about, and she was not about to let anyone question his character.

"I don't know, Maggy," Griffin said, glancing up at her and meeting her gaze and then holding it. "I honestly don't know."

"You make it sound like he had some kind of ulterior motive," she said carefully, feeling her temper begin to simmer.

Griffin sighed. "Maggy, my grandmother is a very wealthy woman, the column notwithstanding. When you add the income from her column and all the other income-producing aspects of life as Aunt Millie, it could certainly inspire some people to try to cash in on a past relationship in order to—"

"You think my grandfather's interested in your grandmother's money?" Shock had Maggy's voice rising several decibels and she leaned across the table, ignoring the looks of the other diners who were suddenly extremely interested in what was going on at their table. "Is that what you think this is about? *Money?*" It figured someone like him would think this would be—could be—only about money.

"I really don't know what to think," he admitted, making Maggy fist her hands under the table.

"Well, Griffin J. Gibson the Third, I'll tell you what I think!" She waited until he looked at her. "I think you're an idiot!"

With that, Maggy slid out of the booth, tossed her napkin to the table and stormed out of the restaurant, leaving Griffin sitting there with his mouth open, staring after her.

"Well, I think that went well," he muttered in disgust before draining his glass of wine and going after her.

Dear Aunt Millie:

My husband and I have been married for almost two weeks. Every day he goes to his mother's for breakfast and dinner. He also spends the entire weekend—from Friday after work until Sunday evening—at his mother's. Is this reasonable behavior for a married man?

Desperate in Detroit

Dear Desperate:

Reasonable? Only if he's married to his mother. It's time for a serious talk with this man—pronto. You need to make it clear to him that having him sleep in your bed but return to his mother's for everything else is simply not an option nor acceptable if he wants to continue to be married to you. You need to explain clearly what you want, need and expect of him and your marriage. If his vision of marriage is not the same, and he doesn't see the error of his ways, then I suggest you send him back to his mother's—permanently. At that point, you should file for an immediate annulment ending this so-called marriage. The longer you allow the situation to go on as is, the longer you will be unhappy, and the longer he will think you are pleased with him and the situation.

Good luck!

Aunt Millie

Chapter Three

"Maggy, wait, please." Griffin had to hustle to catch up with her. "Maggy!"

She was halfway down the dark block before he reached her, gently grabbing her arm to halt her movement.

"Let go of me," she snapped, trying to shake free of him, more annoyed than she could remember.

Traffic buzzed by, headlights flashing against the buildings. In the distance, a siren whined forlornly and a dog barked.

"Please, listen to me." Gently, he held on to her arm, then turned her to face him, dragging her closer to the building—and him—so other pedestrians could pass. "Let me at least apologize. I'm sorry, I didn't mean to insult you or your grandfather, truly."

"The hell you didn't," Maggy said sharply, fire lighting her eyes. "How dare you accuse my grandfather of only being interested in your grandmother's money. That's not just insulting to my grandfather, but to your grandmother as well." She gave his lapel a poke. "You don't even know my grandfather, how dare you make judgments about him or his motives."

"I'm sorry, truly," he repeated. Griffin sighed, realizing for the first time in memory, he was making a mess of a situation he was supposed to be in control of. What on earth was wrong with him? he wondered, glancing into Maggy's eyes.

This woman was having a profound effect on him, scrambling his brains and obscuring his objectives. It was best to get things back under control, the sooner the better.

"Maggy, listen to me. I asked you to dinner so that we could discuss a possible solution to this problem we find ourselves in."

"I haven't heard anything but insults," she said, her temper still simmering. The heat from his fingers, his hand on her arm were wreaking havoc with her pulse and her thoughts. It was hard to think clearly, to keep her temper going when those soft, elegant fingers of his were touching her, making her wonder what it would feel like to have him touch her in other places.

The thought almost buckled her knees.

"Maggy." Griffin sighed again, then glanced down the street so he could get his bearings. "Listen to me. Our grandparents are not going to give up this idea about you taking over my grandmother's column unless we do something to appease them."

"And?" she asked, lifting an eyebrow.

"I think you should come to my grandmother's tomorrow for lunch." He held up a hand when she opened her mouth to protest. "Hear me out," he pleaded, still holding on to her arm so she wouldn't storm off again. "If you go to lunch with her, listen to what she has to say then turn her down, at least she'll feel as if she's given it a shot. Your grandfather as well. Until my grandmother actually meets you, and until you actually talk to her and hear her out, I don't think your grandfather or my grandmother are going to give this up."

"And if I don't?" Maggy asked.

"If you don't, I imagine we'll have a whole lot more nonsense to deal with. Until and unless my grandmother meets you and hears for herself that you have no interest in taking over her column, she's not going to give this idea up." He cocked his head and smiled at her. "Do you honestly think your grandfather will give up without a fight, either? Without trying something else? And who knows how much more trouble they can get into or cause in their effort to make us 'see the light,' 'their' light so to speak?"

Griffin had a point, she had to admit. A good point. She knew her grandfather, and once he got an idea in his head it was stuck there for infinity, unless something drastic changed his mind.

"Just lunch?" she asked suspiciously.

"Honest." He held up his hand. "Just lunch. Meet my grandmother, listen to what she has to say, then once you do, you can tell her yourself that you're not interested and we can both be on our way, and back to our own lives."

"Can I bring my grandfather?" she asked and he grinned.

"Reinforcements, Maggy?" he challenged with a lift of his eyebrow.

"No," she snapped, feeling slightly defensive. "It's just that I want him to hear it coming right from my mouth as well. And besides, if they're together and hear me say I'm not interested, it might go a long way toward deterring them." And just might make her grandfather realize he *had* to stop meddling in her life. Well, she could always hope, anyway.

"Bring your grandfather, then. Shall we say noon?"

She nodded, stepping closer to him and the building to let a group of teenagers pass. "Fine."

"Shall I send a car for you?"

"A car?" Laughing, Maggy shook her head. "What is it with you and cars?" she wondered out loud. "Haven't you ever heard of a cab? Or a bus?"

"A bus," he repeated with such a frown she laughed.

"Never mind." She had a feeling the man had never been on a bus in his life. "We can find our own way there, Griffin."

"I'm sure you can, but I'd feel much better if you let me send a car for you."

Maggy wanted to roll her eyes. This was just another facet that proved they came from two different worlds. He had cars readily at his disposal along with drivers and whatever else he needed to get around town. The thought of taking public transportation was as foreign to him as her having a car and driver available to her.

"Afraid I won't show up?" she challenged, cocking her head to look at him. She saw his eyes darken, turning almost to navy blue, and a skitter raced over her. This man was totally cool and controlled, but from those eyes of his she could tell that there was also a great deal of passion and emotion banked somewhere deep inside. Passion and emotion he kept buried under a very tight lid.

She wondered what would happen if she rattled that lid.

"Are you in the habit of not keeping your word, Mary Margaret?" His voice had cooled considerably, and there was a challenge in his eyes. And being Irish, she never could resist a challenge.

"Are you going to start being insulting again?" she retorted just as coolly, meeting his gaze.

His gaze shifted from eyes, to her mouth, then back to her eyes again, and in that instant he saw the desire that had been simmering from the moment he'd laid eyes on her this afternoon reflected back at him.

It was his undoing.

"Maggy." His voice held a bit of warning, and Maggy stiffened, shifting away from him. Without thought, Griffin pulled her back closer to him, then lowered his mouth to hers, taking what beckoned him, crushing her mouth under his and all but devouring her.

Joy. He'd never felt it before, never felt this insane delirium in his heart or his loins, had never felt as if he was drowning in a kiss and would go willingly to his death for just a bit more.

He'd kissed dozens of women over the years, to be certain, casual as well as passionate kisses, but never had he felt anything that had rocked him and his world as one touch of his lips to Maggy's.

His arms tightened around her, bringing her closer, want to feel the press of her body, the heat of her soft feminine curves rubbing, sliding against the full length of him, anything to stamp out this wild, reckless burst of desire that threatened to incinerate him—them—in one heated swoop.

When he felt her arms creep around his neck, her fingers bury deep into the hair at the nape of his neck, he understood what surrender meant for the first time in his life. At the moment he would have given up anything and everything for her—for this—for what was blazing between them.

He'd always thought himself a calm, efficient man. A man who would never, ever lose his head over something as ridiculous as lust or love. He certainly didn't believe in love. Never had.

Lust was a different story, however. A much different story with Maggy. He'd never felt this type of heat, this intense desire to mate and be one with someone, not ever. He'd quite simply never understood how a man—any man—could be moved to do foolish, ridiculous things simply because of a woman.

Now, at this moment, holding Maggy in his arms, in the middle of a busy downtown Chicago street, he understood, perhaps for the first time in his life, the passion and the power of these kinds of feelings.

And it utterly terrified him.

Ignoring the inner fear that was seeping slowly into his consciousness, he pulled her closer, took the kiss deeper, holding on to her as if he was drowning, and she was the only thing left that could save him.

The feelings storming through him knocked away every single thing he truly ever believed about himself, leaving him shocked and shaking.

Maggy moaned softly as he pulled her closer and deepened the kiss. While it was true she'd never dated much, and Dennis had been her only intimate partner, even then, when she'd been married, she'd never felt the wondrous magic that was seeping through her every pore until this moment—until Griffin.

They seemed to fit perfectly together. His arms so strong and yet so very gentle, he held her as if she was a precious commodity, something to be treasured and protected.

His mouth seduced her, gently prodding, caressing, making her blood sing a heated song as it swam through her veins. Her heart was beating so quickly, so rapidly, she felt her knees go weak. The temptation to hold on, and just let this wicked, wild ride continue forever was strong, and Maggy moaned, pressing herself closer to Griffin, wanting to feel the strength of that strong, hard masculine body against her in an effort to sate this desire.

Maggy's moan seemed to break through the sensual haze. Dazed and nearly dizzy from the range of emotions that had just raced through him, Griffin reluctantly lifted his lips from hers. He saw her eyes, darkened by desire, glittering with need.

Her mouth—that beautiful, sensual mouth—seemed to be beckoning to him again, whispering to him to come closer.

Stunned and appalled at his own actions, Griffin shook his head, trying to shake some common sense into it.

What on earth had he done?

He lifted a hand to his lips. They were still warm and tasted of Maggy. It caused an ache to settle inside low in his gut, making the yearning he'd felt when he'd held her in his arms start anew.

He didn't know what he'd done, but he knew he wanted to do it again.

Now.

And it shook him dreadfully simply because he knew he couldn't.

Not now. Not ever. And for some reason that caused a sharp pain deep inside around his heart.

"I'm so terribly sorry," he said stiffly, discomfited by his complete lack of control. In his entire adult life never had he had anything or anyone shake him like Maggy's kiss. He was quite simply staggered, as if he'd been sucker punched in a courtroom full of people.

Nothing before had ever been able to shake his confidence in himself or his abilities. He was far too disciplined, far too controlled, because watching his father make a fool of himself over the years made him realize he never wanted to lose that control. Losing it made a man look like a fool—especially when it came to women.

And he was certainly no one's fool.

But perhaps for the first time in his entire life, Griffin realized and maybe even recognized the feelings and emotions that had caused his father to behave in such an irresponsible, reckless, not to mention foolish, manner when it came to women all these years.

Because for the first time in his entire life, he'd just felt and experienced those feelings, and he realized they were both intoxicating and addictive.

The experience gave him an entirely different perspective on his father, one he wasn't certain he was comfortable with, because it reminded him that for just a moment—for one brief moment when he held Maggy in his arms—he understood exactly what had propelled his father's behavior with women.

And it terrified him to realize he could be just like his father.

Never, his mind whispered. *Not ever.*

At the moment he felt unsure of his next step, something that had never happened to him before, certainly not in business nor in his personal life. He ruthlessly guarded his emotions to ensure they never entered his personal relationships, knowing that emotions created danger, and dangerous situations caused a man to lose his head. As his father had all these years.

Up until this very moment, he'd been a man who knew what he wanted and went about getting it in a logical, analytical, practical fashion.

He didn't deal with emotions, because they were like

sand, constantly shifting, changing, not something one could ever depend on to remain the same—especially with women.

And in just a few brief moments, here on a busy sidewalk, he'd broken his own cardinal rules for dealing with a woman.

And he had no intention of ever allowing emotions to rule him, his actions or his life. He'd spent a lifetime preparing to prevent that from happening, and he certainly couldn't allow one kiss—one woman—to change his entire vision of himself and his life, let alone his future.

"I don't make a habit of—" He had to stop, take a slow, careful breath, and pray his entire body would stop quaking soon. "I certainly don't go around... I never meant..." He cleared his throat, then ran a nervous hand down his tie to smooth it. "I apologize. I'm not in the habit of... pawing women in public. I mean... this was totally inexcusable, not to mention out of character." It was her fault, he reasoned, knowing immediately it wasn't, but unable to find any other rational reason for his ridiculous behavior. Engaging in public displays of affection was simply not his style.

"Terrific," Maggy said in a shaky voice, withdrawing her arms from around him and feeling suddenly terribly hurt and unbearably bereft. "It wasn't pawing. It was a kiss, Griffin. Just a simple kiss." Although she'd have to admit there was absolutely nothing simple about his kiss.

She was still reeling from it, but looking at him, she had a feeling he hadn't been moved at all. He still looked totally calm, cool and collected.

How could he kiss her senseless, leave her feeling dazed and dizzy, as if someone had just tilted the world out from under her, and then calmly stand there looking totally unfazed?

As if it had been some incidental accident, like stepping on her toe.

Did the man have no feelings?

He had to have icicles running through his veins, she decided, if he hadn't felt anything. They'd generated enough heat to melt the concrete under their feet.

Devastated by his chilly reaction when she'd been so deeply touched made her feel humiliated all over again. Made her realize just how totally different they were.

Clearly, kissing her wasn't something Griffin wanted or enjoyed, nor was it something he wanted to do again, as he'd just made quite clear. Why should she be hurt or surprised, when so many other things about them and their lives didn't mesh?

It just proved once again what she'd believed from the moment they'd set eyes on each other: they were like oil and water, from two different worlds, worlds that could never mesh.

But she'd known that, she realized, so why on earth did it hurt so ridiculously much?

"Maggy—" The bewildered, wounded look on her face tore at Griffin's heart, but he realized he couldn't say anything because for once in his life he had no idea what to say. He'd quite simply never been in this position before and was at a complete loss for words. "Shall we go back to the restaurant and have dinner?" he asked quietly. He took her elbow then dropped it immediately when he felt a flash of need and heat, fearing he'd yank her into his arms again.

"I've lost my appetite," Maggy said quietly.

"I understand completely." He turned to her again in the darkness. Shadows from headlights filtered over her face and he could see the pain in her eyes and knew he'd put it there.

Never in his life had he deliberately hurt a woman, and now, knowing he'd hurt Maggy by being so inconsiderate, by just grabbing her in his arms right out here in public, no doubt embarrassing her, made him feel like a heel.

"It's late, and I did invite you to dinner, which you never even had, so please, at least allow me to have my car take you home?"

"Your car again," she said with a rueful shake of her head.

"Yes, I know you'd much prefer a cab, but I'd feel much better knowing you got home safe and sound in my car."

"Safe and sound," she repeated in annoyance. "You know, Griffin, I'm a fully grown adult, and have been making my way around the city on public transportation for most of my life."

"Indulge me," he said, taking her arm again and all but hauling her to the curb in spite of her annoyance. He lifted his hand, snapped his fingers and a long, black limo slowly sidled up as if by magic.

"How did you do that?" she asked in amazement as the limo slid to a halt in front of her.

"Practice," he said with a smile, glancing down at her. She was standing close to him, close enough for him to smell her sweet, enticing scent. It wasn't vanilla this time, but something just as enticing and powerful, making him yearn to bury his face in the soft, fragrant skin of her neck and satiate this unbelievable ache inside. "Until tomorrow, then," he said, unable to drag his gaze from hers.

"Noon," she said. In spite of the fact that he'd insulted her grandfather and hurt her feelings, Maggy found herself reluctant to leave.

"Yes, noon, Maggy." Unable to resist, and knowing he had to touch her, taste her just one more time, Griffin leaned forward just a bit and brushed his lips gently across hers. He heard her breath catch, felt her hands lift, then cling to the lapels of his suit just as he forced himself to draw back. "Until tomorrow."

The driver, who'd been hovering discreetly behind the trunk, came around to open the door for her.

"Good night, Griffin," she said, more shaken then she'd believed possible as she climbed into the back seat.

"Good night, Maggy." With his eyes on hers, Griffin slowly closed the door.

"Shall I return for you, sir?" the driver asked politely, and Griffin glanced down the street.

"No, thanks. I'll walk." Griffin glanced down the street again, his gaze focusing on a beggar sitting on the ground, leaning back against the building. "I've got something to do first."

Maggy settled back in the seat, watching Griffin as the car slowly waited to pull into downtown traffic.

"What on earth is he doing?" Maggy muttered, watching as Griffin stopped and went down on his haunches next to the beggar to talk to him.

Griffin finally stood up with a nod and a smile, extending his hand as if the elderly man was dressed in an elegant, expensive suit just like his own instead of soiled and tattered rags.

Grinning, the man took Griffin's hand to help himself stand, smoothing a dirty hand down the front of his clothing. Griffin shook the man's hand, then draped an arm around his shoulders and Maggy watched in surprise as Griffin guided the man back down the street, toward the Plantation restaurant, and then escorted him inside.

"Well, I'll be." Stunned, Maggy merely stared after them long after the car had moved into traffic.

And this was a man she thought had no feelings?

Who was Griffin J. Gibson III? she wondered with a

frown, leaning back against the seat. Not many men would accompany a homeless man into one of the most exclusive restaurants in the city, especially not a man who was concerned about propriety or appearances as she'd mistakenly thought Griffin was. Dennis certainly wouldn't have. He'd have simply stepped over the elderly man in an effort to ignore him.

Perhaps she'd been wrong about Griffin, she thought, glancing out the back window, hoping for one more glimpse of Griffin.

He was a man who puzzled and intrigued her. As well as frightened her.

He could just as easily insult her grandfather's character with his suspicious cynicism, and then in the next moment buy dinner for a homeless man.

It didn't matter who he really was, she realized sadly. Because after lunch tomorrow, she was quite certain she'd never see Griffin J. Gibson III again.

So why did that make her so unbearably sad?

Dear Aunt Millie:

Can you help me convince my ma to let me have a gunn? I'm fourteen years old, and reel responsible. I live with my ma and got a best friend named Franky. Franky's fourteen too and his dad just bought him a rifle. Franky and his dad said I could go with them shooting on Saterday if I can get my ma to buy me a gunn. She's a girl and thinks gunns are dangerous, but I know I could handle one and think shooting stuff would be fun. So how can I get her to buy me a gunn?

Charlie in Charleston

Dear Charlie:

Sorry, Charlie. I'm with your mom on this one—and not just because I'm a girl. Guns are dangerous regardless of your gender. Aunt Millie firmly believes you shouldn't have a gun until you're old enough to spell one correctly. Until then, I'd suggest you spend your weekends working on mastering your schoolwork.

Good luck!

Aunt Millie

Chapter Four

"This is so ridiculous," Maggy muttered, glancing at Griffin in annoyance as she waited for Millicent Gibson to open the door to her penthouse apartment. "I don't belong here," she muttered, glancing around and wishing the floor would open up and swallow her.

"Relax," Griffin whispered as Patrick Gallagher, Maggy's grandfather, used his cane to rap on the door to his grandmother's penthouse.

The doorman had already announced their arrival, so Griffin was certain his grandmother would be opening the door shortly. And he didn't want Maggy to bolt. "My grandmother doesn't bite," he soothed with a smile just as the door opened.

"Millicent." Grinning from ear to ear, Patrick leaned his cane against the foyer wall and took both of Millicent's hands in his, letting his gaze take her in. She was still his little Millie, even though her hair was now silver and her

face a bit lined. Age had certainly not diminished any of
her beauty. "You are as beautiful as ever." He lifted her
hand to his mouth for a kiss, and she laughed, her blue eyes
twinkling.

"And you, dear Patrick, are thankfully as full of blarney
as ever." She lifted the hand he'd kissed to pat his cheek
before turning to shrewdly assess, with an approving eye,
the beautiful young woman standing next to her grandson.
"And this must be your darling Maggy."

"That it is," Patrick confirmed with a proud nod, glancing back at Maggy. "Maggy girl, meet Millicent Gibson."

"I'm so happy to meet you," Maggy said with a smile,
taking the older woman's outstretched hand in her own.
"I've heard so many wonderful things about you."

"And I you, dear," Millicent said warmly, keeping Maggy's hand to draw her into the apartment, aware that Griffin
was hanging back, his watchful eyes taking everything in.

"Your grandfather is quite fond of you, you know," Millicent said with a laugh, turning back to glance at Patrick
affectionately. "He's convinced that you're the ideal person to take over my column—"

"Mrs. Gibson," Maggy began.

"Millicent, please, dear," she said, giving Maggy's hand
an affectionate pat. "No one calls me Mrs. Gibson but my
accountant and for what I pay him he should call me Your
Highness," she added with a laugh. "Now," Millicent said,
sensing Maggy's unease and patting her hand in reassurance again as she tucked it into her arm. "Let's talk business later. After lunch. For now, please come in, make
yourself at home."

Maggy tried not to goggle as Millicent led her into the
living room, but it was hard. There were so many beautiful antiques, so many beautiful pieces of art, so many in-

tricate knickknacks, she didn't know where to look first. The apartment reminded her of Dennis's mother's house, where priceless works of arts and antiques vied for space and visual attention.

But Millicent's apartment seemed warmer and much more of a real home than a showplace for wealth. The furniture was actually frayed and worn in spots, as was the exquisite Aubusson carpet on the floor.

"Your home is beautiful," Maggy said in awe, discreetly glancing around. Family photographs adorned nearly every surface, and Maggy noted most of them were of Griffin as a boy.

"Beautiful and a bit aged, I'm afraid," Millicent said with a chuckle as she glanced around. "I've a fondness for things that I've had with me for years and an affection for the familiar." She shook her head a bit. "I probably should have redecorated several times by now, but to be honest, there are so many memories here that I don't think I could bear to part with anything."

Maggy smiled, liking the woman immediately. She was warm, kind and apparently totally unaffected by the obvious wealth that surrounded her.

"Good thing I'm familiar to you, then, lassie," Patrick said with a wink. "Might be you'll want to keep me around for a while as well."

"Might be," Millicent said with a grin. "You never know."

"Grandmother," Griffin said coolly, giving Patrick a look he hoped would intimidate. If Patrick thought he was going to woo his grandmother right under his nose, the old man was sorely mistaken. He still wasn't convinced the man's intentions were strictly honorable, and until he was convinced, he planned to keep a sharp eye on him. "I thought we might have drinks before lunch."

"That's a wonderful idea. Cook should have lunch finished momentarily." Millicent held out her arm for Patrick. "Shall we?" He took her arm and she led him toward the expansive, formal dining room.

Griffin, determined to get through this luncheon as quickly and cleanly as possible for his grandmother's sake, extended his arm to Maggy. "I imagine we should join them?"

She really had little choice in the matter if she didn't want to appear outright rude and embarrass her grandfather. But she looked at Griffin's arm suspiciously, not certain she liked the idea of having to touch him again, not when it scrambled her thoughts and her insides every time she did.

And then of course there was that suspicious way he'd been eyeing her grandfather, as if he thought he ought to count the silver—just in case. It annoyed her to no end.

"I don't bite, you know," Griffin said with a lift of his eyebrow when she hesitated in taking his arm.

"You could have fooled me," she muttered in response. "From the way you've been eyeing my grandfather, I was ready to suggest he get a tetanus shot."

"And what is that supposed to mean, Mary Margaret?" Griffin asked.

Maggy came to a halt, and turned to glare up at him. Their eyes met, held, then clung, an arc of awareness sparking between them, nearly frying the air floating between them.

Blinking the effect away as her body seemed to warm and hum, Maggy had to swallow several times in order to find her voice.

"What that means is that you'd better watch your step when it comes to my grandfather," she snapped, eyes blazing and narrowed. "I'll not have anyone hurt or harass him." She gave him a poke in his expensive tie. "And especially not some fancy dandy who thinks himself better than us."

"Fancy dandy?" Griffin repeated with a shake of his head, desperately trying not to be amused at her quaint terminology. He wasn't entirely certain what fancy dandy meant, it certainly hadn't been covered in law school, but he was quite certain she'd just insulted him. "Now, Mary Margaret—"

"I told you not to call me that," she snapped, giving him another poke as temper sizzled on her tongue. She wasn't certain who she was more annoyed at—him because of the effect he had on her or herself because her body was betraying her by reacting to him purely on a feminine, physical basis.

"Sorry," he said quietly, all but mesmerized by her flare of temper and what it did to those incredible emerald eyes.

Unable to draw his gaze from hers, when she licked her lips, his gaze shifted to that beautifully shaped, unpainted mouth and he remembered how she'd tasted last night. Desire, like an unrepentant snake, reared its ugly head, and the urge to lower his head and brush his lips against hers, to taste her again and satisfy this unbelievable craving that had begun the moment he'd laid eyes on her was nearly overwhelming.

"I apologize," he said stiffly. "You did ask me not to call you that." He had to clear his throat, then slipped a hand in his pocket so he wouldn't haul her into his arms again. "Shall I call you Maggy, then?" he asked, lifting his free hand to adjust his tie and wondering why his voice sounded strained, even to his own ears.

In spite of her temper, or maybe because of it, Maggy couldn't seem to draw her gaze from his, either. His eyes, those incredibly glorious blue eyes of his, were quite firmly looking at her mouth. It made her lips twitch, ache in a way that made her want those lips on hers again. But he'd already made it clear he wasn't interested in her or in kissing her, hadn't he?

Stunned by her own thoughts, Maggy dug deep for what was left of her temper and annoyance.

"I hope after this lunch you won't have reason to call me anything at all," she snapped, miserable and sorry she'd ever agreed to this fiasco in the first place.

"Well, at least we're in agreement about something," Griffin said as he took her arm and all but hauled her into the dining room, ignoring the muttered curses she aimed at him under her breath, hating the fact that under it all, his touch was making her pulse pound like a jackhammer.

"So tell me a little about yourself, Maggy," Millicent said after lunch had been served, the table cleared and coffee poured.

A bit flustered at being put on the spot, Maggy glanced down at her coffee cup then at Millicent. "There's not much to tell. I'm twenty-eight, work for my grandfather at the deli, live at home and take classes at night to finish my degree—"

"Yes, your grandfather mentioned that," Millicent said, causing Maggy to glare at her grandfather suspiciously, wondering just how much of her private life he'd been discussing with people. "What are you getting your degree in?"

"Communications," Maggy said. "I only have another semester to go, and I'll be done."

"Good." Millicent nodded, then sipped her coffee. "I understand from your grandfather that you originally dropped out of school in order to get married." Deliberately, Millicent made her voice soft and sympathetic. Patrick had already told her this was a sore point with Maggy, and she had no wish to embarrass the young woman, merely to see where she was in her life.

Aware that Griffin's face had changed, his gaze had sharpened on her, Maggy nodded, not really interested in getting into the specifics of her failed marriage.

"Yes, that's true." Maggy shrugged, then went on simply because Griffin was staring at her, his coffee cup poised in midair as if waiting for the other shoe to drop. She merely glared at him with a warning look that said back off. Forcing a smile, she turned to his grandmother.

"I'm afraid I was much too young and far too foolish to make a decision about a lifetime commitment," Maggy said with a lift of her chin, trying not to let the burn of embarrassment show through. She hated having to admit to failing at anything, especially something as important as marriage, particularly since she'd always believed marriage was sacred. "It didn't last," she added quietly.

With a quiet nod, Millicent set her cup down and gave Maggy her full attention, sensing the young woman considered this a personal failure. "Sometimes, Maggy, we learn life's greatest lessons from our perceived failures." Millicent laughed. "Believe it or not, I had a brief, disastrous marriage myself very early in life."

"Grandmother!" The shock on Griffin's face would have been comical if Maggy hadn't seen the quick burst of hurt beneath it. She didn't particularly like the swell of sympathy she felt for him.

"Now, Griffin," Millicent said quickly, reaching across the table to pat his hand. "Don't look so shocked, dear. It was a very long time ago, long before I even met your grandfather." Millicent sighed, then sipped her coffee. "It's not something I'm proud of, no women ever is," she said sympathetically, glancing at Maggy. "Which is why I've never mentioned it. We don't like to admit what we perceive as personal failures, but sometimes in our youth our judgment about men is about as solid as an uncooked egg." Smiling, she glanced at Maggy, a totally understanding feminine look that communicated volumes. "It's never pleasant to admit that we've been wrong about a man we believe we love."

Griffin continued to stare at his grandmother. Never had he imagined that his grandmother had been married before. What else, he wondered, didn't he know about her? It was odd, until today, until he'd met Maggy and Patrick Gallagher, he would have bet his business that there wasn't anything he didn't know about either of his beloved grandparents.

And he'd have been wrong, he realized dully, staring morosely into his coffee cup.

"In fact, it was right after my disastrous marriage that I met your grandfather, Maggy." Millicent turned to Patrick, then laid her hand over his, making Griffin's eyes narrow when Patrick linked his fingers through hers and held on.

Griffin caught Maggy's look and decided if he wanted to get through this luncheon with his shins intact and unbruised, he'd probably better be more careful about hiding his feelings, or rather his suspicions, about her grandfather.

Millicent shook her head before continuing. "I was sorely in need of a job and a place to live since I had far too much pride to go home to my parents after my marriage failed." She sighed, then shook her head in good humor again. "Ah, the stupidity of youth."

Patrick lifted her hand and kissed it. "Nay, Millicent, you were never stupid."

"No, you never made me feel I was, Patrick," she said

fondly, turning her attention to Maggy. "Your grandfather gave me a job in his deli, and a place to live." Smiling, her eyes twinkled. "And more importantly, he gave me his friendship."

"You *lived* with this man?" Griffin burst out in a tone that had Maggy rolling her eyes.

"Not *with* him, Griffin dear," Millicent pointed out carefully, tempted to roll her eyes in exasperation just as Maggy had. "Above him. Patrick lived in the first-floor apartment of the same building he lives in now. I lived on the second floor. I actually lived there and worked in the deli until I met and married your grandfather," she explained, looking at Griffin. "In fact, it was in Patrick's deli that I met your grandfather."

"You met Grandfather in a *deli?*" Griffin hadn't meant for his tone of voice to be quite so harsh, but he was just surprised by his grandmother's admission.

Millicent chuckled. "Well, Griffin darling, an Irish deli is quite a respectable place of business." Millicent's eyes twinkled. "Even all those years ago. You needn't act like I announced I met your grandfather in a strip joint."

"Grandmother, you've never been in a strip joint," Griffin pointed out stiffly.

"Don't be so certain of that, Griffin darling."

Totally amused, Maggy hid a smile behind her coffee cup, still feeling a bit of sympathy for Griffin who was all but choking on his coffee. The poor man looked utterly stunned and quite miserable. If he wasn't so serious, he'd probably realize his grandmother had been kidding. She hoped.

"Now, Maggy, tell me, do you read 'Aunt Millie'?" Millicent asked, extending her cup to Griffin for a refill.

"Every day," Maggy admitted, watching Griffin pour his grandmother's coffee with a shaky hand. "I wouldn't miss it."

"Good." Millicent considered for a moment. "You know, Maggy, I wasn't much older than you when I created the column. I was scared to death at first," Millicent admitted with a chuckle. "I was very young, had just come out of a disastrous marriage, didn't have a college degree yet." Sipping her coffee, she shook her head. "It's one thing to give advice to family and friends but quite another to know that millions of people are reading every word you write. At the time it seemed like an awesome responsibility, particularly since my confidence was pretty low." She shrugged. "I couldn't imagine how I could be expected to tell others how to live their lives when I'd made such a mess of my own."

Realizing Millicent had just voiced her own sentiments, Maggy leaned forward. "Then how and why on earth did you do it?"

Millicent smiled. "The why of it is easy. I don't have a lot of patience for nonsense," she admitted with a smile.

"Sounds just like my Maggy girl," Patrick muttered into his coffee cup, then snapped his mouth shut when Maggy shot him a warning look.

"Nor did I understand how people could be so lacking in common sense about so many things, especially love and marriage," she said, aiming a pointed look at her grandson, who had the good grace to flush. Millicent turned back to Maggy. "I had made a mistake with my marriage, yes, but that was because I had ignored my own inner warnings, and stubbornly went ahead with the marriage even though everything inside me was telling me it was wrong."

"I know how that feels," Maggy muttered, realizing she'd done the same thing.

"But at least I recognized from the beginning it was a mistake." Millicent shrugged. "I made the wrong choice, which is far different from not having the common sense to know it was wrong from the beginning."

"I think I understand exactly what you mean," Maggy concurred, smiling at Millie.

"I'm sure you do." Millicent paused. "When the newspaper publisher first approached me, I knew his son from the neighborhood, I was quite certain this was not something I was interested in or even capable of, but like you, Maggy, I had been giving advice and solving problems for my friends and family for years. The column simply seemed like just an extension of that. So that's the how of it. As for why?" Millicent chuckled again. "I'm Irish, Maggy, and was blessed with a strong sense of pride, and at an age when I believed that I could do anything. Originally the job was mine on a thirty-day basis, just a trial to see how it went. In spite of everything, I knew I had to do it if only to prove to myself that I could. Pride wouldn't let me do otherwise," she added with a smile. "And the rest, as they say, is history."

"Some history," Maggy said with a shake of her head, impressed. "You've done a remarkable job."

"I've had help, dear. I have expert consultants all over the world that I can tap into if ever a subject comes up and it's over my head or out of my league, everyone from NFL officials to Nobel Prize physicists to voodoo priests."

"Voodoo priests?" Maggy repeated with a laugh. Millicent nodded.

"I'm not an expert on anything except human behavior. That fortunately hasn't changed in the forty-odd years I've been doing the column. After that, well, I'm afraid I need a little help now and then." Cocking her head, she looked at Maggy shrewdly. "Now, you say you read 'Aunt Millie' every day?"

"Yes."

"Good. Then I wonder if you'd do me a favor, Maggy."

"Anything," Maggy said, perplexed but meaning it. Her affection for Millicent was immediate and genuine. In some ways, she reminded Maggy of her own beloved grandmother.

"Maggy, I know you haven't had time to digest the idea of taking over my column." Millicent held up her hand to stop Maggy's stunned protest. "Please, let me finish." Millicent took a deep breath then went on. "I know this idea isn't something that you've had time to really seriously consider, for that matter. I mean how could you when you just learned of the possibility a day ago? However, it's something I've been looking into for a while." Millicent leaned forward, giving Maggy her full attention. "I'd like to give you a letter that 'Aunt Millie' received. Read it, and then tell me what your response would be. Will you do that for me?"

"Now?" Maggy asked, feeling her nerves jitter at being put on the spot in front of everyone.

"Yes, please." Millicent reached under her place mat and extracted a neatly folded letter. "'Aunt Millie' received this yesterday. I'd like you to read it and tell me what advice you'd give to this young woman."

Aware that everyone at the table was watching, Maggy took the letter and slowly read it. "Well," she finally said with a frown when she'd finished reading, "first of all, I'm a big believer in accepting responsibility for your actions— right or wrong."

"Good. Good," Millicent said, beaming at Patrick behind her coffee cup.

Maggy's eyebrows drew together in concentration. "And if I understand the situation clearly, this nineteen-year-old college student was raised in a very strict moral and religious household and knew her parents' views and expectations regarding premarital sex long before she ever met or dated her boyfriend of four years." Maggy paused thoughtfully for a moment. "Although I don't condone her mother's snooping or invading her daughter's privacy by ransacking her room, the fact that she did, and found the girl's birth control pills, doesn't absolve the daughter from her responsibility in this, either."

Millicent nodded thoughtfully. "Okay, Maggy, but the young girl says that since her mother has found the birth control pills she's called her vile names and told her that she must promise never to have relations with her boyfriend again, or she must move out. What would you recommend that the daughter do?"

Maggy thought about it for a moment. "I think it's pretty clear. If she's living under her parents' roof, she has to abide by their rules whether she agrees with them or not. If she can't abide by the rules, she's going to have to move out—for all their sakes." Maggy shrugged. "It's part of the consequences of both the mother's and daughter's actions. The mother shouldn't have been snooping, nor do I think she should have engaged in vile name-calling once she discovered her daughter was sleeping with her boyfriend. I don't condone using the cover of religious beliefs to be deliberately cruel to anyone, especially your own children. As for the daughter, she knew her parents' views on premarital sex before she engaged in it, and she had to know if her parents found out there would be consequences. Knowing that, she still chose to disobey her parents' house rules and these, quite simply, are the consequences. If she wants to continue to have relations with her boyfriend, she's going to have to move into her own home where she'll be able to make her own rules. If she wants to continue living in her parents' home, she's going to have to abide by their rules." Maggy shrugged. "I think it's that simple."

With a smile and a flourish, Millicent reached under the other side of her place mat and extracted another folded sheet of paper. "This is Aunt Millie's answer. It will appear in next week's paper. Would you mind reading it, Maggy?"

Maggy slowly began to read, her nerves jumping with each word. "Okay," she finally said. "Even though our words are perhaps different, our intent, content and advice is basically the same."

"Mmm, yes they are, aren't they?" Millicent said with a pleased smile.

"Yes, but that doesn't mean I'm interested or qualified to take over your column, Millicent," Maggy protested, feeling trapped.

"Perhaps," Millicent concluded, eyes twinkling as she turned to Maggy in challenge. "Are you afraid, Maggy?" she asked softly, and Maggy could feel heat suffuse her cheeks.

"Afraid?" Pride kicked in hard and strong. Maggy's chin went up, her shoulders straightened. She never could resist a challenge. "Of course not!" She would die before she ever admitted the idea simply terrified her. "I'm not in the least bit afraid." Lord, her nose was going to be two inches longer before this luncheon was over if she didn't stop telling fibs.

"Good." Millicent nodded. "Then what I propose is that you give me—and the column a thirty-day trial. The same as I had when I first started. I think, Maggy, that's fair. My instincts about people are pretty sound, and my instincts about you are that you have the passion and compassion, as well as basic understanding of human nature, to handle my column. If I didn't feel it, we wouldn't be having this conversation." Millicent cocked her head, a challenge in her eyes. "So what do you say, Maggy? Are you willing to give me thirty days?" Millicent shrugged. "What could it hurt?"

Feeling trapped, Maggy glanced around the table. Her grandfather looked proud and hopeful and she wanted to groan, knowing she could never knowingly disappoint him.

Her gaze shifted to Millicent, who looked totally relaxed and confident in what she'd just proposed.

Maggy made the mistake of looking at Griffin, and saw the distrust and suspicion in his narrowed eyes. Her temper, never totally controlled under the best of circumstances, flared then ignited.

"Fine, I'll do it," Maggy said, deliberately glaring at Griffin. "But only for thirty days," she added firmly.

"Fabulous, Maggy," Millicent said. "Absolutely fabulous. I'm delighted." She leaned over and kissed Maggy's cheek. "We'll start first thing tomorrow. We'll do what's called 'shadowing.'"

"Shadowing?" Maggy repeated nervously, not at all certain what that entailed.

Millicent nodded. "It merely means you'll follow me for the next thirty days both at work and at social events—anywhere Aunt Millie must appear. That way, you'll get a complete understanding of what this job entails. And since you'll need an escort, Griffin can shadow you," Millicent added with a smile.

"Social events?" Maggy said dully. Then, realizing what Millicent had added, her eyes widened and she glared at Griffin. "*He'll* be shadowing me?" she repeated weakly, feeling as if she'd just been sentenced to thirty days of hard labor. With the wicked warden watching her every step.

"Mmm, yes dear. You absolutely must have an escort for social events and situations, and since Griffin's been escorting me since his grandfather's death, it only seems logical for him to continue the practice with you, don't you agree, darling?" Millicent had turned to Griffin, who looked as if he'd just swallowed a mouse. His face was pasty, his lips pursed, his eyes all but bulging.

"Griffin?" Millicent said with a lift of her eyebrow.

"Um, yes, Grandmother," he said when he finally found his voice. "I agree." He never could refuse his grandmother anything. But the thought of spending the next thirty days in such proximity to Maggy was enough to give him pause. The woman did things—strange things—to him and his body, not to mention his mind and his manners.

How on earth was he going to handle this? he wondered dismally, staring broodingly into his coffee. He lifted his gaze, looked at Patrick, and then Maggy, wondering what on earth had caused her to change her mind.

Suspicion began to wind its way through him. She'd told him she had no interest in his grandmother's column. None at all. Now, here she was agreeing to take it over for thirty days.

Why? he wondered, feeling once again as if he'd been sucker punched. Like Marissa, Maggy had told him one thing, when, in fact, she apparently had every intention of doing another.

He couldn't help but feel a grudging bit of disappointment in Maggy. He thought she was different, thought she had both loyalty and integrity.

Apparently he'd been wrong.

"Good. Good. Now darlings," Millicent said with a smile, "we'll start first thing tomorrow morning." She turned back to Maggy again, ignoring the scowl on her grandson's face. "Since there's a large society charity ball Aunt Millie has to attend tomorrow evening, the first item on the agenda is to get you some proper clothes."

"Clothes?" Maggy repeated weakly, glancing down at her plain cotton dress.

"Yes, dear. And I've already made an appointment at my spa. They expect you at nine for a full body treatment and makeover."

"Body treatment and makeover?" Maggy repeated. She was beginning to feel like a rather dumb ventriloquist, repeating everything Millicent said merely because it was far too much for her to take in all at once.

She had what felt suspiciously like a severe tension headache clustering behind her eyes. The mere idea of being trussed up and fussed over was more than enough to give her a headache.

"Yes, dear," Millicent said. "Griffin can give you the details while your grandfather and I enjoy a walk along the lakeshore." Smiling, Millicent bent over and gave Maggy another peck on the cheek. "I'm so relieved, Maggy dear, and confident you're going to do a wonderful job." Millicent laid a gentle hand to Maggy's cheek. "Don't worry," she whispered softly. "It's going to be fun."

Fun? Maggy looked across the table to Griffin. His jaw was tense and a vein in his forehead was throbbing. Maggy rubbed the now full-scale throbbing at her forehead. She had a feeling she was going to spend the next thirty days trying to fight her attraction to Griffin while trying not to strangle the arrogant man!

Dear Aunt Millie:

I work nights and my husband works days. We have two small children ages eight and ten. We deliberately arranged our work schedules so one of us would always be home with our children. It's worked very well for the past eight years. However, two months ago a very young, attractive divorcée moved in next door. I didn't even know my husband knew her, until last week. I came home from work midshift with a migraine, to find my husband gone and a twelve-year-old—our neighbor's daughter—at my house with my sleeping children. I was livid. My husband returned home around two in the morning, casually explaining he and Missy—our neighbor—occasionally go out for a drink in the evening and leave her daughter to sit with my children. Needless to say, I'm hurt and furious that my husband never mentioned this, nor did he bother to tell me that he'd been going out with this woman. I think this relationship is highly inappropriate. My husband claims he did nothing wrong, that they're just friends and I'm overreacting. I don't think I believe him. What should I do?

Concerned in Cleveland

Dear Concerned:

Friends? Hmm, Aunt Millie has heard this kind of relationship called many things, but friends isn't one of them. Aunt Millie is afraid when someone protests they did nothing wrong—and haven't told their spouse or significant other about it until caught and forced to fess up—invariably they know darn well what they've been doing is wrong and simply want to avoid facing the consequences of their misdeeds. Not an admirable quality I'm afraid. Now, since your husband deliberately withheld this information from you, you have good reason not to believe him. Aunt

Millie is a firm believer that an omission is the same as a lie—one simply not voiced. Now, as for what to do, you have several options. The first is to tell your husband that his middle-of-the-night drinking forays with this neighbor—as well as any other woman—has to stop. Immediately. Second, leaving your small children alone in the middle of the night with a twelve-year-old was reckless and is not to be repeated. Finally, I'd tell your husband that the two of you arranged your schedules for the benefit of your children. If he has a problem with your working nights, and can't find something to do to entertain himself without involving another woman, you'll quit your job. If it comes to that, Aunt Millie is afraid you have a more serious problem than your husband's choice of middle-of-the-night…friends.

Good luck!

Aunt Millie

Chapter Five

Maggy waited until Millicent and her grandfather had left the penthouse before trying to talk to Griffin.

"I know what you're thinking," she said quietly, glancing down at her coffee cup.

"Do you now?" he asked.

"Your face is an open book," she commented. "I know you think I lied to you, that when I said I wasn't interested in your grandmother's column—"

"Yes," he replied coolly, "that's the way I seem to remember it. But apparently you *are* interested," he said, lifting his cup to drain it, then setting it down with more force than necessary, nearly shattering the fine bone china.

"No," Maggy said with a sigh of her own, resting her chin in her hands. "I'm not interested in her column. Not really," she added with a frown.

"I see." He lifted his gaze to hers and saw the hurt and confusion in her eyes and decided to soften his stance and his voice, and give her a chance to explain. "If you're not seriously interested in taking over my grandmother's column, than why did you just agree to do it for the next thirty days?"

"Because I simply couldn't refuse her," Maggy said vehemently. She pushed to her feet, then turned to stare out the long, floor-length windows that afforded a beautiful view of the Chicago skyline, feeling both annoyed and frustrated with him, herself and the situation. "Your grandmother's quite a woman," she said absently, trying to gather her thoughts.

"I know that," he said softly. He'd stood to move right behind her, and now she could feel his body heat warming her. She shivered unconsciously.

"Did you see the expectant, hopeful way they were looking at me? As if I were a chocolate brownie and they were both starving chocoholics?"

Griffin laughed, he had no choice. She was right; his grandmother was quite a formidable woman. He could never refuse her anything, so how on earth had he expected Maggy to? Especially when his grandmother was so determined, as she'd been today.

"Yes, I must admit, Maggy, they were both looking at you like that. And I must also admit I was grateful I wasn't the one under their scrutiny."

Maggy nodded. "I simply couldn't bear to hurt them." She shrugged. "I figured if I agreed to do this for thirty days, if I at least gave it a chance, that would convince them both once and for all that I wasn't right for the job."

He turned her to face him. "So what you're saying is that you're *not* really interested in my grandmother's column?"

Maggy tipped her head to look up at him, then blew out a breath because looking at him made her pulse trip erratically again. "I have to admit the job does sound interesting, parts of it anyway, but there are parts I could sorely do without."

"Such as?" he asked. Slowly and wondering why he couldn't resist touching her, he began to knead her shoulders, noting she was tense.

"The social stuff." Maggy all but shivered. "I cannot even bear the thought of being decked out and trotted out like some Christmas decoration on display. I know I'll enjoy the part where I can help people, but it's the other—stuff—the social stuff—that's going to drive me nuts."

"Is that how you think of social events?" he asked quietly, realizing he'd felt the same way himself over the years but felt duty-bound to escort his grandmother, particularly since his grandfather's death.

"Yes," she admitted, meeting his gaze. "I'm not interested in becoming part of Chicago's high society."

"No, I imagine you're not," he said with a smile, lifting a hand to brush a stray curl off her face. She was far too honest and forthright to ever become part of that social circle where diplomacy and tact were rated first and honesty and truthfulness a poor second. "I honestly can't see you putting up with all the pretentious nonsense that goes on at these affairs."

"So why do you do it?" she asked, confused. And he smiled that heart-tugging smile that had her almost catching her breath.

"Pretty much for the same reason you're going to be doing it," he admitted.

"For your grandmother?" she asked, totally surprised.

"You sound shocked, Maggy."

"I am." She laughed suddenly, realizing his hands had slipped from her shoulders to her waist. She could feel the heat and warmth of his hands even through the thin cotton fabric of her dress. "I guess I just expected you to enjoy those social gigs where you could mix and mingle with those of your own ilk."

He chuckled softly, shaking his head. "Maggy, you make me seem like some kind of elite social animal." He settled his hands more comfortably around her waist, drawing her a bit closer.

"I guess that's the way I saw you," she admitted with a rueful shake of her head. There were so many things she'd believed him to be, and now, as she got to know him, was finding out he wasn't. It was confusing, she realized, as were her feelings for him. And the situation.

"You know, Maggy, not everyone who has money is a snob."

"Oh, I know that, Griffin." She smiled. "My grandfather has money. Oh, not on the scale of your grandmother I'm sure, but more than enough so that he's quite comfortable. But he doesn't have a snobby bone in his body."

"No, you're right. He doesn't." *Snob* wasn't quite the word he'd use to describe Patrick Gallagher. And he had a feeling his idea of financially comfortable and Maggy's were probably a bit different. Another thought had Griffin frowning. "Did you see the way they looked at each other?" he asked worriedly.

"I did," Maggy said, smiling. "I can't remember when I've seen my grandfather look so happy."

"I know," he said. "My grandmother as well." He shifted his gaze back to hers, saw her mouth beckoning to him and willed himself not to kiss her. "I don't think I've seen my grandmother smile like that since before my grandfather passed away."

"Really?" The thought pleased Maggy and she grinned.

"Really," he confirmed. "It was nice to see her so animated," Griffin admitted with a sigh. "She just looked so happy and excited. It's been a long time since she's been that way."

"And it pleased you, didn't it?"

"Yes," he reluctantly admitted. "It did. I want her to be happy, Maggy. She's done so much for me, given me so much, I can't bear the thought of her being unhappy." That didn't mean he wanted her vulnerable to someone taking advantage of her, though.

"But it still worries you that it's my grandfather who is apparently making her so happy?"

Griffin was no dummy. He knew when to keep his mouth shut, and knew this was one of those times. Rather than answer Maggy, he simply drew her closer, then lowered his mouth to hers, wanting—needing—to touch her, to taste her once again.

He heard the warning signal clanging in his ear, but ignored it, concentrating only on one thing, the woman in his arms.

His lips touched hers gently, carefully, waiting to see if he'd imagined that incredibly intense feeling.

He hadn't.

It raced through him like a raging river, hot and fast, burning away any thought or protest he might have had. He tightened his arms around her, drawing her closer until he could feel the rapid thrumming of her heart, steady and soft against his, as he took the kiss deeper, feeling needs and wants surface with a force that rocked him.

Maggy heard his soft, wistful sigh, and simply moaned out a sigh of her own as his mouth, his clever, beautiful mouth played over hers, coaxing a response until she wound her arms around him and gave in to the feelings storming through her, feelings she wasn't certain she wanted to acknowledge. Or worse, knew how to handle.

"Ah, Maggy," he whispered, resting his cheek against hers until his heart and body settled. "So," he said quietly, brushing his lips against the silk of her hair. "Tell me about your husband."

"My husband?" Stunned, she shook her head and tried to laugh, glancing up at him, aware that his body was still pressed against hers. "Where on earth did that come from?"

"I've been wanting to ask you since you mentioned it to my grandmother, but I didn't want to pry or embarrass you." It had been driving him crazy, knowing Maggy had once belonged heart, body and soul to another man, a man who hadn't had the good or common sense to keep her. How on earth could a man let someone like Maggy go? He simply couldn't understand it.

"But it's okay to pry now?" she asked, making him laugh.

"Yeah," he said with a laugh of his own. "Tell me about him."

She sighed, wrapped her arms more tightly around his waist and, leaning against him, enjoying his warmth and support. "There's not much to tell, really. I met Dennis when I was a sophomore in college. He was a senior, prelaw. He came from a very prominent, wealthy East Coast family. Of course, at the time I fell in love with him I didn't know that."

"Would it have made a difference?" Griffin asked quietly.

"I'm not sure," she admitted. "By the time I did find out, though, it was too late."

"You were already in love with him," Griffin said quietly, feeling a surge of jealousy flare out of nowhere again.

"Yeah." She frowned, brushing her hair off her face. "Or at least I thought I was," she said with a painful laugh.

"Right after he graduated, he asked me to marry him. He was planning on attending law school at Notre Dame and wanted me to go with him."

"And you did?"

She nodded. "Yeah."

"What happened, Maggy?" he asked quietly, holding on to her more tightly.

She shrugged. "His family was horrified that he'd married me, someone who was not even in the same social stratosphere, let alone financial stratosphere, so they cut off all financial aid to him. I dropped out of school to support us so he could finish law school."

"You gave up your own education for his?" Since he'd never known a woman could be so unselfish, her sacrifice totally astounded him. Never, in his experience, had he ever met a woman like Maggy. A woman who put someone else's needs ahead of her own, without thought, without regret. She was, he decided, one unbelievably incredible woman.

"He was my husband," she said a bit defensively. "And marriage is—and was—something sacred. At the time I believed you got married for life. You do what you have to do to make it work. If you love someone, it's not work, it's just part of life."

Griffin nodded, digesting her words, wondering how she could still have such faith in an emotional system that had already failed her once. It just proved his theory about emotions not being stable or permanent.

"What happened?"

"Within three months of his law school graduation, Dennis announced that I no longer fit into his lifestyle. That he really needed a wife who was more sophisticated and worldly, that I just didn't really fit him or his life." She shook her head. "He was right, you know," she admitted with a small smile.

"No," Griffin corrected, lifting her chin to force her to look at him. "He was an idiot." Eyes darkened by anger, he gave a brief nod, amazed and confused by the emotions swirling through him like a cyclone.

How was he going to handle the next thirty days with her, and keep his sanity and his emotions in check?

Carefully, his mind whispered. He'd handle the next thirty days in the same meticulous way he handled everything else in his life: very, very carefully.

She was late.

The next afternoon Griffin glanced at his watch with a frown. The hot lunch-hour sun beat a heated pattern down on his custom-tailored navy pinstriped suit as he paced the sidewalk in front of his private club.

He detested tardiness. It showed a distinct lack of courtesy and consideration for others, one he was quite unaccustomed to enduring. No one dared waste his time.

He glanced at his watch again. How on earth long did a makeover take? he wondered in exasperation. It was now close to one in the afternoon. He'd made reservations for a twelve-thirty lunch. Much to his annoyance, twice he'd been forced to go inside and beg the pardon of the maître d' for his tardiness, pushing back their reservation by fifteen minutes each time, hoping by then Maggy would show up.

But here it was, close to a half an hour later, and he was still pacing and waiting for her. The woman was, quite simply, deliberately trying his patience, Griffin thought. And there was no excuse for it.

Griffin sighed and paced faster, trying to rein in his

temper. He rarely allowed it free rein, but at times it did have a mind of its own. And this was apparently one of those times.

Griffin frowned suddenly, supremely agitated as he slipped his hand in his pocket to finger his change, pondering the problem that had occupied most of his day, and unfortunately had helped foul his mood.

His grandmother and her relationship with Patrick Gallagher.

Unfortunately, his grandmother was apparently already besotted with Patrick, as evidenced by the fact that Patrick had arrived early this morning with a dozen calla lilies and a taxi to take his grandmother out for the day—which was why Griffin was stuck in the hot sun waiting to have lunch with Maggy instead of his grandmother.

And explained his foul mood. He'd been brooding about the situation all day, knowing his grandmother was off with Patrick doing who knew what. And he didn't like it. Not at all. It wasn't that he disliked Patrick Gallagher—he didn't really know the man—but the fact of the matter was he was still suspicious of Patrick's timing and his motives.

The fact that Patrick had been writing to his grandmother since his grandfather's death only seemed to solidify that Patrick was trying to inch his way into his grandmother's life—and her bank account. He'd probably had no idea she had a grandson, and expected it to be smooth sailing to capture a wealthy, grief-stricken widow.

When his grandmother announced her retirement, as well as the search for her replacement, Patrick probably figured he could kill two birds with one stone—woo his grandmother for her money, and get a nice fat job with plenty of financial benefits for his granddaughter.

Well, Patrick was apparently in for a rude surprise since

Maggy wasn't interested in taking over his grandmother's column, which solved one problem. Now, what to do to protect his grandmother's fortune was another.

A rapid-transit bus pulled to the curb, huffing and puffing gusts of filthy, fetid fumes. Blinking rapidly to disperse some of the fumes from his eyes, Griffin turned suddenly and collided hard right into a woman who'd just gotten off the bus.

"I'm so sorry," he said quickly, reaching out to grab the woman's arms to steady her. "How clumsy of me."

Maggy chuckled. "You haven't had a clumsy moment in your life, Griffin."

His head lifted; his eyes widened and he merely stared. The voice was Maggy's, definitely. He couldn't miss the sarcasm. But the body...the hair...the face. His eyes widened further and he simply, utterly goggled at the incredible woman standing in front of him.

Her hair had been cut almost as short as a boy's along the sides, and was now slicked sleekly back against her head, giving her an elegant, sophisticated look. The front had been left curly, tousled in a way that made her look incredibly sexy, as if she'd just stepped out of bed.

He frowned slightly. Something had been done to the color as well. Around her face, her hair was a lighter shade, almost a pale blond that accentuated not just that beautiful skin, but those incredible emerald eyes as well. She had some kind of smoky color all around her eyes, and her lashes seemed to have grown an inch, giving her a sultry siren look.

Then his gaze slid to her mouth and he almost lost his breath. That beautiful full mouth was now outlined in one color, emphasizing the lush fullness, then filled in with something clear and shiny, making him ache to taste her again. It was, he decided, the most incredible transformation he'd ever seen.

"My God, Mary Margaret," he said as he continued to hang on to her arms and absorb the fact that this incredibly beautiful woman *was* Maggy. "What… What…have you done to yourself?"

He saw the quick flash of hurt, and then the stricken look that settled over that incredibly glorious face, and immediately felt contrite and regretful. That hadn't come out quite the way he'd meant it. But she'd thrown him completely and totally off balance.

"I didn't do anything, buster," she snapped, giving him a poke in his designer tie and not giving him a chance to explain. "It was that fancy salon you sent me to that did it." Self-conscious now, Maggy touched a hand to the back of her hair, mortified.

Griffin's reaction had her feeling both angry and defensive, not to mention foolish, that she'd gone along with this ridiculous makeover to begin with. She was perfectly happy with the way she looked before she'd had all this nonsense done to her, nonsense that apparently wasn't quite the improvement she'd thought if Griffin's face and attitude were to be believed. She wished she didn't feel quite so disappointed.

"Maggy, listen, I didn't quite—"

"Stuff it, buster." She stepped around him to stomp away, furious and embarrassed. She wanted neither his apology nor explanation. She didn't need anyone telling her that someone like him would never approve of, or for that matter, accept her. Hadn't she learned that lesson with Dennis? Nothing she did was ever acceptable or good enough for a man like her ex-husband.

Clearly, Griffin was just another bird of the same feather.

And it didn't matter, she told herself, furiously blinking back hot stinging tears. Didn't matter at all.

"Maggy, please don't walk away when I'm talking to you." He reached out and caught her arm, turning her toward him, more annoyed with himself than with her.

"Don't tell me what to do," she said, trying to shake free of him without much success. She wished he'd quit staring at her. It only made her feel more self-conscious. As if she'd been playing dress-up in order to fit into some role someone else had assigned to her.

Still staring at her, Griffin felt as if someone had tied his tongue into a slipknot. She'd been beautiful before in a simple, uncomplicated way.

Now, whatever she'd had done to herself had merely enhanced her features to the point of breathtaking. That was the only word he could think of. He simply couldn't take his eyes off her.

He felt it again, that quick swipe of desire so strong, so swift it brutally knocked him off his equilibrium until he felt like a schoolboy encountering his heart's desire.

Annoyed and totally unnerved by his response, he dug deep for some of his noted control. He strove for some balance and, realizing neither was possible at the moment—not while he was looking at her, or touching her— he allowed the anger that had been simmering just moments before she arrived free rein. It was the safest emotion at the moment since he didn't trust anything else he was feeling.

"You're late, Mary Margaret," he complained, deciding to leave the subject of her appearance alone lest he make a fool of himself. Again. He'd give his emotions time to cool and then explain his comment. "More than half an hour," he added, tapping his watch.

"Big deal," she said, struggling to hold on to her dignity in spite of her bruised feelings and simmering temper.

"There's simply no excuse for tardiness. It's the height of rudeness, not to mention inconsideration."

"I had to wait for the bus. It was late so I was late." Her pulse was thrumming in rapid tempo. The warmth and softness of his fingers on her bare arms was sending her heart and body into a rapid, rabid tailspin.

"The bus," he repeated with a deep frown as if he didn't quite comprehend the word.

"Yeah, the bus," Maggy repeated. If she wasn't so annoyed at him, she would have laughed at the expression on his face. "You know, public transportation with lots of everyday people like me, you know, average working people." She leaned closer, realizing she was annoying him and enjoying it. "You know, a big machine that huffs and puffs smoke. Ever heard of it, pal?"

It took a moment for her words and her meaning to sink in. "Do you mean to tell me I have been cooling my heels, waiting outside in this heat simply because you decided to ride the *bus?*" He looked so horrified, she did laugh. "Where on earth is the limo I arranged for you?" he asked, glancing up and down the street as if expecting the limo to magically appear out of thin air at any moment. Anything so that he wouldn't have to keep looking at her. It was scrambling his brains.

"I ditched it," she said, shrugging her shoulders. "As well as the driver. Told him to go play hooky."

His temper went from simmer to sizzle in a heartbeat and he jerked her closer until her body bumped his.

Maggy felt a flash of heat and a quick flash of unbridled desire, startling her.

"You ditched it?" he repeated in stunned shock. He dropped his gaze to her mouth, and found his pulse accelerating. His palms grew damp as the feel of Maggy's sweet, soft bare skin warmed him, making him ache, making him yearn.

And that mouth of hers. It seemed to be beckoning him, as if silently whispering…taste me, taste me.

He was heartily afraid if he didn't get himself back under control, and quickly, he might just do it.

Annoyed at him for his behavior, and herself for responding, Maggy slapped both hands to the front of his chest. She detested that he was chiding her as if she was irresponsible, when she'd never done an irresponsible thing in her life. She was late because of the appointment he'd arranged! "Listen, buster—"

He dragged her closer, bumping the toe of her sandals with the tips of his shoes. "No, *you* listen," he said, still staring at her mouth. Yesterday, it had been soft and unpainted. Today, it glistened silkily.

Her lips were parted slightly in anger, and her eyes, those glorious emerald eyes, were sparking flashes as bright as any jewel. "You were given a limo not only for your convenience, but for everyone else's as well. As Aunt Millie you have a responsibility to act in a mature, responsible manner, not like a spoiled, irresponsible brat."

"Who are you calling a brat?" she snapped, clenching her fingers into fists and crumpling the lapel of his custom suit with them. Her heart was hammering so loud from his nearness she feared he'd hear it.

"You." He struggled to rein in his emotions to no avail. He'd been drawn as taut as a tightrope since he'd laid eyes on her. "You are exasperating and unnerving—" Without thought, Griffin jerked her close to him, then lowered his mouth to hers, taking what beckoned him, crushing her mouth under his and all but devouring her.

"Maggy." Her name came out half plea, half prayer,

and he mightily feared he was losing his mind. She was stealing his senses with every touch, every breath, and he didn't seem able to stop or prevent it.

His arms tightened around her, bringing her closer, wanting to feel the press of her body, the heat of her soft feminine curves rubbing, sliding against the full length of him, anything to stamp out this wild, reckless burst of desire that threatened to incinerate him—them—in one heated swoop.

When he felt her arms around his neck, felt her response as wild and unbridled as his own, he only dragged her closer, took the kiss deeper, not caring that they were standing in the middle of a busy Chicago street, in full view of lunchtime commuters and diners.

All that mattered, all he could think of, was Maggy and the desire racing through him.

Maggy moaned, pressing herself closer to Griffin, wanting to feel his touch, the press of him everywhere, anywhere to stamp out this blazing fire that he'd ignited the moment he'd touched her.

Maggy's moan seemed to break through the sensual haze. Dazed and nearly dizzy from the range of emotions that had just raced through him, Griffin reluctantly lifted his lips from hers. He saw her eyes, darkened by desire, glittering with need.

"Maggy—"

She held up her hand, knowing the drill already. "Let me guess. You're sorry and it won't happen again, right?" she said in exasperation, trying to get her breathing back under control.

Stunned, he stared at her. "Yes, that's right," he said stiffly, frowning.

Maggy sighed, then blew out a breath, trying not to feel

hurt by his reaction to kissing her. Clearly he liked it, but apparently because of who she was, or who he was, kissing her didn't fit into what he considered acceptable social behavior.

So what else was new? she wondered. Dennis hadn't found her acceptable on any level, either.

"That's exactly what you said the first time you kissed me. That you were sorry."

"I see," he said. He hadn't realized he'd been repeating himself. "But I am sorry, Maggy."

"And it's not going to happen again, right?" She tried not to hold her breath, praying for once, just once, he'd admit he enjoyed kissing her.

"Correct," he said, knowing even as he said the word that it was a lie. Not kissing Maggy would be like not breathing. It was quickly becoming very necessary to his well-being, and for the life of him he simply couldn't figure out why. He took a cautious step closer to her. "Maggy, please forgive my inexcusable behavior this afternoon." With a sigh, Griffin slid a hand through his hair. "You look beautiful," he finally admitted with a smile, laying a hand on her cheek. "Absolutely beautiful."

"I do?" Self-consciously, she lifted a hand to her newly styled hair and looked at him suspiciously, wondering if this was just a tactic to distract her from his kiss.

"Yes, you do." His fingers gently stroked the tender skin of her face. "I guess I was just taken aback when I first saw you and I'm afraid I let my foul mood get the best of me."

"It did that," she agreed with a smile, willing to forgive him and feeling so much better about how she looked now.

He chuckled. "I guess I just didn't expect such a drastic change."

"But you do like it?" she asked hesitantly, still not certain.

"Like it? You're beautiful." He took her hand and twirled her around in a circle. "Isn't she beautiful?" Griffin asked a passing female shopper, making the woman smile and nod at her.

"Griffin!" Mortified, Maggy yanked on his hand, pulling him close to her. "Stop soliciting compliments from strangers."

"But why?" he asked with a grin, looking as if he was about to do it again.

"Because it's embarrassing," Maggy admitted with a smile of her own. "I'll take your word for it."

"Will you now, Maggy?" he asked quietly, his gaze steady on hers. She could feel her pulse kick up at the look on his face. And for the first time in her life, she truly felt beautiful. When he looked at her like that, she had no other choice.

"Yes, Griffin," she admitted with a wide smile. "I will."

"Good." He slid his arm around her waist. "Then can we please go have lunch? I'm starving."

"Griffin," she began hesitantly.

"What now, Maggy?"

She lifted his arm and glanced at his watch. "I'm sorry, I can't. I don't have time. I have an appointment with your grandmother's personal shopper in less than a half hour and it's all the way on the other side of Michigan Avenue. If I don't leave now, I'll be late." She straightened, deciding to mimic him. "And that would be rude and infuriating."

He was struggling not to smile. "Yes, I agree, it would be." He sighed then glanced around. "All right, but do you promise me you'll eat something? Every time I invite you out for a meal you never seem to get to eat."

"I promise," she said, holding up a hand as if giving an oath.

"Good. And take my car. You'll never make it on time if you have to wait for a cab or bus." Griffin lifted his hand and signaled, and just like the other night, a large, black limo pulled to the curb.

"I'll be staying for lunch, so you won't have to worry," he assured her, and she smiled. "I won't need the car."

"All right, all right."

He glanced at his watch again. "Now, remember, Maggy. I'll pick you up promptly at six. We have that gala benefit tonight." He managed a smile. "Your first social appearance shadowing my grandmother."

"Don't remind me," she muttered, getting nervous just thinking about it.

"Six, Maggy?" he repeated, and she nodded.

"Fine. Fine." She leaned up and kissed him on the cheek. "Thanks, Griffin."

"For what?" he asked, touching his cheek where she'd kissed him.

"For...everything."

"Okay."

"Oh, and one more thing."

"What's that?" he asked as the limo driver got out to open her door.

"Don't nag, it drives me crazy," Maggy said, staring at his driver and wondering why he looked so familiar. It wasn't the driver Griffin had had the other night; he'd given *her* that driver this morning, so why did this guy look so familiar? she wondered.

"Then don't be late," he countered.

"Griffin, do I know this driver?" she asked with a frown, confused.

"Know him?" Griffin asked with a frown of his own, turning to look at the man, who got back inside the limo when Griffin opened the door for Maggy himself, and she slid in. "No, I don't think so. I just hired him." He shut the door firmly, checking to make sure it was closed properly. "I'll see you later this evening then," he said, leaving over the open window."

"At six and I'm not to be late because it's rude, inconsiderate, and irritates the hell out of you," she said with a smile, making Griffin laugh.

"Exactly." Griffin tapped the roof of the car to let the driver know it was safe to pull out.

Maggy watched Griffin out the window until he disappeared from view, then sighed and relaxed back against the leather seats. She glanced at the driver again, certain she'd seen him somewhere. She never forgot a face.

Then it hit her and she leaned forward, tapping him gently on the shoulder.

"Sir, excuse me, may I ask you a question?"

"Yes, ma'am," he said, grinning at her in the rearview mirror. "But you can call me Ernie."

"Ernie…did you…uh…have dinner with Mr. Gibson at the Plantation the other night?" If she wasn't mistaken, this was the homeless man who was sitting on the sidewalk when she'd stormed out of the restaurant that night. The same man she'd seen Griffin talking to, and then walking into the restaurant with as she pulled away.

His grin widened. "Yes indeedy," he confirmed with a nod of his bald head. "I certainly did. Mr. Gibson treated me to a fine, fine dinner."

"He did?" Maggy said in amazement.

"Yes, ma'am, and when he found out I used to be a truck driver but I'd lost my job when the trucking firm went under, he asked me if I wanted to drive for him."

"Drive for him?" Maggy repeated, a little stunned.

Now she understood why Griffin had insisted she take a car. It wasn't because he was being a snob or arrogant, it was because he'd given Ernie a job driving, and since he already had a driver, he'd given Ernie the job of driving *her* around.

Maggy's eyes slid closed and she realized she'd completely and totally misjudged Griffin. Again.

"Yes, ma'am," Ernie confirmed with a happy nod. "And come the first of next month, I'll be getting me my own apartment as well. Right now I'm staying in a fine room right over at the YMCA."

"And did Mr. Gibson have something to do with that as well?" Maggy asked with a smile, and he nodded again.

"He surely did, missy. When he found out there was a two-year wait for subsidized housing, well, him being a lawyer and all, he just made a few phone calls and next thing I know I got me my own apartment come the first of the month and a room at the Y until then." Ernie stopped for a red light, then turned to her, grinning broadly, revealing one gold incisor. "Mr. Gibson, now he's what I call good people. Yes indeedy. He promised that in a month or so, once I got some time on the job, he's going to talk to the court to see about getting me some visitation rights with my grandson." The man's face sobered, but his eyes were dreamy. "I ain't seen my grandboy in almost two years. Not since I hit that spot of bad luck and lost my job."

"What happened?" Maggy asked softly, and he sighed.

"Well, my daughter and I never did get along once her mama passed, and I guess she was ashamed of me being jobless and homeless and all. Didn't think I was a good influence on the boy."

"No, I'm sure that's not true, Ernie," Maggy said, patting his shoulder in comfort, horrified by his words. How could anyone be ashamed of their own family, and more importantly, how on earth could his daughter sit by and not help her own father?

It was unconscionable.

"It's true," Ernie confirmed with a sad shake of his head. "But my grandson, now, he and I, well, we've always been tight. Boy's one heckuva fisherman, I'll tell you. Being able to see him again, why, it's more than I ever hoped for." He nodded his head, then stepped on the gas. "And Mr. Gibson says with a little time and luck I just might be able to see him again. He's good people, Mr. Gibson is, ma'am, he truly is. I praise the day I ran into him, yes indeedy, I surely do."

"That was very kind of him," Maggy said softly. Griffin *was* a wonderful man. A man who may have seemed like her ex-husband but was as different inside as an egg to an artichoke.

With a happy sigh, Maggy crossed her legs, then glanced out the window, realizing that she just might have another problem on her hands.

How on earth was she going to protect her fragile heart from Griffin? The *real* Griffin she was suddenly beginning to know? Maggy shook her head, realizing she didn't have a clue.

Dear Aunt Millie:

My husband and I recently took early retirement and moved to a beautiful town house in Arizona. Our development has a private pool for residents' use, which my husband and I frequently enjoy. Yesterday, one of our neighbors, also retired, had a female visitor, a rather young female visitor, who also had a very large black Labrador with her. This woman pushed the dog into the pool, and then the two of them proceeded to play and frolic in the water for several hours. I'm not a puritan, but I don't think dogs ought to be swimming in our pool. We've since learned this woman is our neighbor's—although she looks young enough to be his daughter or granddaughter. My husband doesn't want to make waves by complaining to our neighbor, but I don't feel comfortable swimming in the pool knowing that it's being used by someone's four-legged friend. What should I do?

Retired in Rockford

Dear Retired:

Although Aunt Millie loves animals, I'm afraid that you are correct to be alarmed by this situation. Dogs can transmit staph infections to humans quite easily, and if a dog with a staph infection is swimming in your pool, everyone who swims in that pool is risking exposure. Clearly your neighbors must know that dogs shouldn't be swimming in that pool, so talking to them directly will seem like a confrontation and might create a problem far bigger than the one you've got now. Certainly your town-house association must have rules regarding pets and the pool. My first call would be to them. If a call to your townhouse association doesn't rectify the problem, my next call would be to the county health department, which I'm sure will have more than a thing or two to say about your frolicking four-legged friend. I do believe that will put a stop to this situation.

Good luck!

Aunt Millie

Chapter Six

"Bloody hell, I'm late. I'm late. Blast it, I'm going to be late. Again." With a weary sigh, Maggy barreled through the back door of her apartment, arms laden with shopping bags, all but ignoring her brother Michael and grandfather who were sitting at the kitchen table having a Guinness.

"Maggy girl, don't you have a minute to say hello to your brother?" her grandfather asked with a grin, his eyes widening in pleasure at the change in her appearance. His heart warmed and he felt a strong bit of Irish pride. "Maggy girl, what's this you've done to yourself?" her grandfather asked with a twinkle in his eyes.

Maggy came to an abrupt halt, then flushed, lifting an arm weighted down by shopping bags to touch her hair, still a bit self-conscious about her new look. "Do you like it?" she asked cautiously.

"Aye, lass, it's stunning." Patrick winked at her. "You look as beautiful as your grandmother on the day that we wed."

"Oh, Grandpa." A quick flash of hot tears caught her off guard, but home and family were her weaknesses, and so very necessary to her life and well-being. "Thanks, Grandpa."

"Aye, you're welcome, lassie." Her grandfather lifted his glass and took a sip of his beer, eyeing her over the rim of his glass.

"Hi, Michael." She bent and planted a loud, smacking kiss on her brother's cheek, then frowned at him. He was dressed completely in black, from his T-shirt to his jeans and boots. His sleek black hair was pulled back into a stub of a ponytail, and his face was covered with several days' growth of black stubble.

He had his shoulder holster on and it held some lethal-looking weapon that looked large enough to stop a rhino at a hundred feet, only adding to his scurrilous appearance. There was a small diamond winking in his left ear and a slim gold chain with a cross hanging around his neck.

"You look like a pirate," she said with a laugh. "Working undercover again?"

"Yeah." Slouching low in his chair, with his long legs stretched out under the table, Michael grinned up at her, a grin that had stopped a fair share of female hearts.

She reached out a hand and rubbed one of his wide, broad shoulders. "You look tired." His huge green eyes were shadowed with fatigue and his shoulder was tense under her fingers.

"I'm beat," he admitted around a huge yawn, reaching for his own glass of beer and taking a sip. "I've been working almost around the clock for the past week."

"Michael," she said, frowning as worry settled in. "Is this case dangerous?"

He laughed, then gave her hand an affectionate tug. "Sweetheart, I'm a cop. It's the nature of the beast."

"Are you being careful?" she asked, biting her lip and wishing her brothers had become something safe like accountants.

"I'm always careful, sis, you know that," he said with a lazy grin, letting his gaze take her in. "Looking pretty fancy there, kid," Michael said. "Going highbrow on us now, Maggy?"

"Stuff it," she said good-naturedly, grabbing a piece of cheese off the snack plate in front of him as he reached for his beer. "Michael, I thought you were bringing over someone for dinner," she said, glancing around the kitchen. "Someone Grandpa fixed you up with?"

"Please don't remind me," Michael said with a groan, slouching lower in his chair and glaring at his grandfather.

"What? What! What did I do?" Patrick inquired innocently, drawing back to place a woeful hand on his heart. "Is it a crime now to want my grandchildren happily wed? To give me great-grandbabies to warm my lap and my heart in me old age?"

"No," Michael admitted, trying to hide his amusement. "But if you were going to fix me up with someone, Grandpa, the least you could have done was make sure she was at least someone near childbearing age." Michael turned to Maggy with amusement dancing in his eyes. "Sara Riley, the woman Grandpa fixed me up with, dropped by the station house today. Luckily, the desk sergeant tipped me off."

"Not what you expected?" Maggy asked, trying to hide her grin. Her grandfather's blind dates were notoriously ill matched and ill suited, but that never stopped him. He was persistently persistent, much to their chagrin.

"Well, let's just say Ms. Riley didn't need a date, she looked more like she needed a doctor and an oxygen tank.

She had to be sixty if she was a day," Michael said with a grin and a shake of his head.

Terribly affronted, Patrick straightened his shoulders defiantly. "I'll have you know, Michael Callahan Gallagher, that Sara Riley is not a day over…sixty," Patrick finished weakly, making Maggy and Michael laugh.

"You're incorrigible, Grandpa," Maggy said, kissing her grandfather again. Nervously she glanced at the clock once more. "I've got to run. Griffin will be here in twenty-eight minutes and the man's as punctual as Big Ben."

"So I heard you're considering taking over the 'Aunt Millie' column." Michael said casually while her grandfather pretended to be seriously interested in the contents of his beer glass.

"*Considering* is the operative word, Michael," she admitted, glancing pointedly at her grandfather. "It's merely a thirty-day experiment. After that, I'll make a final decision. I've got my first social gig as Aunt Millie tonight." She rolled her eyes. "That's why the new hairdo."

"Looks good, kiddo," Michael said with a grin. "You'll knock 'em dead." Michael circled his glass with his finger, trying to be casual. "Grandpa tells me Millicent Gibson's got a grandson?"

Uh-oh. Maggy had heard that macho-male protective tone many, many times in one of her brothers' voices, in fact every time she went out with a male.

"Don't even go there," she said firmly. "Griffin is not someone I'm dating." Only kissing, her mind whispered, but she ignored the small voice, trying to put Griffin's kisses out of her mind. "This is strictly a business arrangement, Michael, nothing more, nothing less. Truly. So don't go getting all macho and protective on me."

"Who, me?" Michael asked innocently, casually letting

his hand come to rest on his gun. "Have I ever been macho and protective, Grandpa?"

"Nay, laddie, not so as I noticed," her grandfather answered, shaking his head, then smiling into his beer so Maggy couldn't see.

"Griffin is a seriously stuffed shirt, Michael, not one to understand six macho males in the throes of a testosterone temper tantrum over their sister." She sighed, not liking the look on her brother's face. "Michael, please?"

"Will you stop worrying, kid? You worry too much. Would I ever do anything to embarrass you?" he asked, chucking her under the chin and making her scowl.

"Do I have to answer that?" she asked with a laugh. "Just promise you'll…behave."

"I'll behave," he said, lifting his hand in the air as if taking an oath.

Relief sagged through her. She had absolutely no idea how Griffin would react to the sight of her six brothers confronting him. "Thanks." She kissed his cheek again. "I've got to run." She started out of the kitchen again. "Grandpa, when Griffin gets here can you stall him a bit, give me a bit more time?"

"Aye, I'll do my best, lassie."

"Thanks."

With Ernie and the limo waiting at the curb, Griffin impatiently paced the length of the Gallaghers' living room, waiting for Maggy. Her grandfather had let him in a moment before escaping out the back door to pick up his grandmother.

Griffin wasn't certain if he was relieved or alarmed that Patrick was escorting his grandmother to the gala tonight. It made him very nervous to have the man spending so much time with his grandmother, but at least he'd be able to keep a close eye on him.

Griffin glanced around the spacious room with the wide windows across the entire front, which afforded a bird's-eye view of everything going on in the street below.

The furniture was well-worn and comfortable, giving the room a homey feeling. Atop almost every surface were family pictures taken over the years. There was a lingering scent of some meal still hovering in the air. It wasn't unpleasant, merely a reminder that this was truly a family home where people lived and loved, shared experiences and their lives.

He wandered over to a table and picked up an old photograph. It was only when he brought it closer that he realized it wasn't that old.

Maggy was sitting in the middle of the photo, smiling, surrounding by six men who towered over her, all with matching grins. These had to be her brothers, he thought with a smile, noting the uncanny resemblance of the men.

And there was Maggy, sitting among them like a delicate, fragile flower with her strawberry-blond hair, a sharp contrast to her brothers' darkness, and those glorious green eyes glittering brightly. The two men standing behind her each had a large protective hand on her shoulder, dwarfing her in comparison.

They all looked so happy, he thought a bit wistfully, wondering what it would have been like to have siblings. Particularly brothers. He'd always wanted a brother, he recalled, wanted to share that kind of familial experience, but unfortunately, like everything else that had to do with family—he'd been disappointed.

"Griffin?"

He turned and bobbled the frame, almost sending the

picture crashing to the floor. His breath backed up in his throat, and he had to remind himself to breathe.

Maggy stood before him like some beautiful pagan goddess. She wore a slim floor-length column of black in some kind of knit that clung to every single inch of her in a way that only emphasized her curves and delicate, feminine figure. The skimpy little straps of the dress bared her shoulders and arms, and he saw a smattering of freckles across her delicate shoulders. They were adorable.

Her gown was simple and unadorned, yet it was the sexiest, most elegant, sophisticated dress he'd ever seen. On any other woman it would have looked plain, but on Maggy it simply looked fabulous.

Around the pale, slender column of her neck she wore something chunky and ebony to match her dress. The contrasting darkness against her fair skin nearly made his breath hitch again. The necklace picked up the light with her every movement, sending shards of brilliant sparks outward. She wore matching ebony stones at her ears.

His gaze took in the length of her. Beneath the hem of her dress, pale pink-painted toes peeked out from sexy, strappy sandals that matched the dress perfectly. Tossed casually over one arm was a matching ebony shawl.

Determined not to make the same mistake he had this afternoon, Griffin took a long, deep breath before attempting to speak. He had to swallow hard to get the words out, then carefully, with hands shaking, set the picture back down on the table, fearing he'd drop it if he didn't. Then he turned and gave her his full attention, not caring if his actions appeared as smooth as a befuddled eight-year-old's.

"You look…beautiful." He had to swallow again. "Absolutely, utterly beautiful." He had an urge to bundle her up and hustle her back into her room, not wanting to share this beautiful woman with anyone, let alone the collection of male vultures who would be attending this charity gala tonight.

Maggy had no experience with these kind of people. He could only hope she'd be able to handle herself. His jaw tightened. If not, he'd make sure he stuck close to handle them for her.

"You like my dress then?" she asked a bit nervously, glancing down at herself self-consciously and feeling unbearably pleased at his compliments. "I know it's pretty plain, but—"

He crossed to her and took both her hands in his, noting that sometime in the last twenty-four hours her bitten-down nails had grown and were now elegantly polished in the same pale pink shade as her toes. She had, Griffin realized, absolutely beautiful hands. Fragile, a bit frail and as feminine as any he'd ever seen. Soft as a rose petal, too, he thought, absently rubbing his thumb against her palm, feeling an unexplained need to touch her.

"It's perfect on you, Maggy." Still holding her hands, he drew back to look her over from head to toe. He was beginning to feel the stirrings of that gut-swiping lust that had snuck up on him and scrambled his wits the moment he'd laid eyes on her.

He had to get a grip on himself. His reactions to Maggy were totally unprofessional, and this was simply a professional relationship and a temporary one at that, as he'd been reminding himself for several days.

So it was totally inappropriate for him to have kissed her, or allowed anything of such a familiar nature to develop between them.

It had taken him hours to settle down this afternoon,

making him nearly useless since he couldn't stop thinking of the taste of her, the touch of her, knowing he wanted—needed more.

Unfortunately, he couldn't allow it for many, many reasons. Although looking at her now, he seriously doubted he'd be able to keep the promise he'd made to himself. He was only human, after all, and faced with this beautiful woman it was hard to stop the need to touch her, especially now, knowing what bliss it would bring.

"It's just perfect, Maggy."

"Good." She let out a breath she hadn't known she'd been holding. She was so nervous about how he'd react to the clothing she'd chosen, fearing he'd be critical and judgmental as he'd been when he first saw her new hair and makeup.

His opinion shouldn't be so important to her, she knew, but it was, and Maggy knew she was playing with fire, and she had no wish to walk into the flames ever again.

"Are you ready?" Griffin asked with a smile, and she nodded. "Good. The limo's waiting." He took her hand again, absently rubbing the tender skin, making her shiver, then grinned when she moaned and muttered under her breath. "Maggy, why on earth do you dislike riding in a limo so much?" he asked as he led her by the hand toward the back door.

"I don't know," she admitted. "It just seems so pretentious. The car is so big and long, not to mention black, and it just attracts so much attention. Everyone stares at it as if expecting the Queen of England to get out." She shrugged as he held her arm to help her down the back stairs. "It just makes me uncomfortable." Then she remembered Ernie and his new job. "But I guess I can handle it for the next thirty days."

"Yeah?" he asked, surprised and pleased.

She turned to him with a grin. "Definitely."

"Terrific," he said with a grin of his own as he opened the back door of the limo for her before Ernie could get out. Watching Maggy slide in, her dress slid up, revealing a hint of long, slender thigh.

Griffin felt his pulse kick into overdrive and he closed his eyes and said a quick, fervent prayer.

Professional, he repeated over and over silently, trying to ignore the way his body was responding just to being near Maggy. He had to remain totally, completely professional. He simply was not a man to let emotions overrule his common sense.

He glanced at her again and felt his resolve weaken.

He'd be professional, he told himself through gritted teeth. Or die trying!

Leaning against the bar in the elegant ballroom with the melodious notes of the orchestra drifting softly through the air, Griffin sipped a straight Irish whiskey and kept an eagle eye on Maggy.

Since they'd arrived three hours ago she'd been surrounded by people anxious to meet, question and get a good look at Aunt Millie's potential replacement.

Surprisingly, Maggy had handled herself very well, Griffin thought with a hint of unexplained pride. She was gracious, charming and very patient. She also had a wicked sense of humor that had kept more than a few men entertained and certainly piqued their interest, much to his chagrin.

"Griffin darling, there you are." Millicent extended both hands to her grandson, then smiled at him. "Are you having a good time, dear?" she asked, letting go of one of his hands to link her arm through Patrick's.

"Yes, Grandmother. It was a lovely evening." He'd never tell her how much these gala society bashes bored him to tears.

"Where's Maggy?" Patrick asked with a lift of his eyebrow, wondering if perhaps there was some trouble brewing since the lad was at the bar all alone.

"On the dance floor," Griffin said with a nod toward Maggy.

"Aye, yes, I see now." Patrick frowned, figuring he might as well stir up the pot a bit to see what…popped up. "Who's that handsome young lad she's dancing with?" he asked, turning back to Griffin and almost smiling when he saw a flare of heated jealousy flare in his eyes. Instead, he gave Millicent's hand an approving squeeze.

"Snorky Golden," Griffin said with just a hint of disdain, eyeing the man holding Maggy in his arms. If Snorky held Maggy any tighter to him, Griffin decided he was going to cheerfully charge the dance floor and punch the man's lights out.

"What's a Snorky?" Patrick asked with a confused frown, making Griffin laugh.

"That's his name, Patrick." Griffin sipped his drink, keeping an eye on Maggy over the rim. "He's from one of the oldest, most prominent investment banking families in the country." The man was also just a bit too full of himself, Griffin thought.

"Aye, 'tis fine, son, but they couldn't give him a regular name like Bob or Tom perhaps?" Patrick asked, still confused and wondering why anyone would hang a silly name like that on a child.

Griffin laughed again. "That's his nickname. He's a champion snorkeler, thus the name."

"Aye, I see," Patrick said, still frowning, not really seeing anything of the kind.

"Darling," Millicent said. "It's late and I'm afraid I'm quite tired. Do you mind if Patrick sees me home now?"

"Of course not, Grandmother," Griffin said, bending to kiss her cheek. "Go home and get some rest."

"And you'll see Maggy safely home, dear?"

"Of course."

Millicent turned toward the dance floor with a pleased smile. "She was wonderful tonight."

"Mmm, yes she was," Griffin had to admit, glancing at Maggy still clutched in Snorky's arms.

"She absolutely charmed everyone," Millicent said, exchanging a sly smile with Patrick. It was clear from Griffin's expression that he was not pleased that Maggy was dancing with another man. Perhaps there was hope for her grandson after all.

"She's done that as well, Grandmother," Griffin said, not taking his eyes off of Maggy.

"I couldn't have been prouder of her." Millicent watched her grandson's face. "She's compassionate, articulate, bright—"

"Beautiful," Griffin murmured absently, unaware of the pleased, conspiratorial look Millicent and Patrick exchanged.

"Yes, dear, she's beautiful as well." Millicent patted her grandson's check. "I'm glad you finally noticed," she said with a gentle laugh, drawing Griffin's gaze. He blinked to clear his thoughts.

"What, Grandmother?" He shook his head. "I'm sorry, I didn't hear what you said."

"Never mind, it's not important." Supremely pleased, she kissed his cheek again. "I'll see you tomorrow, dear. Have a nice evening."

"I will," Griffin muttered, shifting his gaze back to Snorky, whose hands had begun to intimately roam Maggy's back.

Griffin's eyes narrowed dangerously as he watched Maggy's eyes widen in alarm. She squirmed, trying to move back and away from Snorky and his roving hands.

Jealousy and anger blew up out of nowhere again, surprising Griffin. He was not and never had been a jealous man, not with any woman. But for some reason the sight of Snorky pawing Maggy was enough to haze his vision with a combination that had him seething inside.

Snorky had no right to put his hands on Maggy. None at all. Slamming his drink to the bar, Griffin crossed the dance floor in quick strides, dodging couples, then tapped Snorky on the shoulder.

"My turn, pal," he said quietly, watching relief flood Maggy's face.

"It was a pleasure, my lady," Snorky said with a deep-waisted bow. "I hope to do it again sometime."

"Not in this lifetime," Griffin muttered, all but knocking the man over as he nudged him out of his way to slide his arms protectively around Maggy. The moment he drew her close, he felt the heat of her body seep into his, which made him instantly aware of her.

"Thanks," Maggy said in relief, clinging to Griffin.

"Are you okay?" he asked, leaning back to study her face. Her scent was once again playing havoc with his senses, making him want, making him yearn.

"You mean because of that octopus?" Relaxing against him, she smiled, absently laying her tired head on Griffin's shoulder. "I'm fine. He thinks he's a Casanova," she said in amusement.

"And you don't quite see him that way?" Griffin asked as he guided her around the dance floor.

"No, I think I see him more as the court jester," she admitted with a grin. For some reason her words brought a sense of relief and Griffin felt himself relax.

"You're tired," he murmured softly, inhaling deeply of that wonderful scent.

"Yeah, I am," she admitted with a deep sigh before glancing up at him.

In her heels, she came to just under his chin, and when she lifted her head, her mouth—that beautiful enticing mouth of hers—was bare inches from his. Griffin had to swallow hard when he realized that all he had to do was dip his head a bit in order to touch his lips to hers.

"Did you have a good time tonight?" he asked, trying to force his mind to keep up polite conversation so he wouldn't do something foolish. Like kiss her again. It was bad enough he was holding her close, feeling her lush, feminine body slide and move against his with every step. His blood seemed to be heating to a dangerous level.

"Yes, thank you." Deliberately, Maggy shifted her gaze over his shoulder. It was very hard to be this close to Griffin, to respond to him the way her body was responding and know that the feeling was not reciprocated. His message had been delivered quite effectively and repeatedly.

He'd already made it clear he didn't enjoy kissing her, and as if that wasn't enough, the way they constantly rubbed the wrong way against one another told her that this was not the kind of man with whom she could ever have any kind of future. He came from *this* world, she thought, glancing around the elegant room, where women draped themselves in diamonds and furs and dripped sophistication as easily as laughter.

She could dress the part, she could play the part, but it

wasn't her. It never would be. She'd learned that lesson with Dennis and still had the heart-scars to prove it.

"Are you sure you had a good time?" Griffin asked with a lift of his eyebrow.

"I'm smiling still, aren't I?"

He drew back from her to study her face, then grinned. "Actually, Mary Margaret, that looks more like a grimace than a smile."

She laughed softly, giving her head a toss. "It probably is. My feet are killing me," she said with a groan. "I don't know how women walk in heels. They're so high I'm surprised I didn't get a nosebleed. The minute we're out of this place, off they come. And I'm starving," she admitted, sighing, letting herself relax against him.

"You didn't eat much of your dinner and I know you didn't have lunch."

"Smothered chicken," she said, drawing back to look at him. "It's bad enough they wanted me to eat that, did they have to tell me how they killed it?"

Laughing, Griffin hugged her tighter. "What do you say we take off and get you something to eat?"

"Could we?" she asked so quickly, so hopefully, Griffin laughed again.

"Absolutely. I don't know what's still open, but I'm sure we can find something."

"I'm not fussy." She pressed a free hand to her tummy, glancing up at him. "Not at this late hour. I just need something to tide me over until morning." His mouth was oh so close and so very, very tempting. Just thinking about the taste of him, the way he made her feel, Maggy had to desperately fight the urge to stand on her tiptoes and kiss him again.

He was not, she'd again realized this afternoon, quite the cold, calculating man she'd once thought him to be. Beneath that icy, arrogant facade was a man who cared deeply for others and for his family, something that had moved her deeply.

"Great. Let's get out of here." Taking her hand, he guided her out of the ballroom, pausing to grab her cape off the back of her dinner chair, gently draping it around her shoulders as he waved good-night to several people.

The moment they stepped out into the luxuriously carpeted lobby, Maggy toed off her high heels, then heaved a relieved sigh, wiggling her toes.

"Oh, that's so much better," she said, bending to pick up her shoes and juggling to keep her cape on at the same time.

"Maggy, are you planning on walking barefoot through the lobby and out to the car?" Griffin asked in amusement.

"Well, it's preferable to crawling, Griffin," she said. "And there's no way I can put these blasted heels back on again." She glanced up at him with a lifted eyebrow. "Am I embarrassing you? I know this isn't very professional."

From the look on his face she had a feeling most of the women who attended this type of society shindigs probably didn't walk around these elegant surroundings barefoot. But she wasn't one of those women, she was her own person and had no intention of changing for anyone.

"No, you're not embarrassing me," he said with another laugh. "But I don't want you to hurt yourself or step on anything." Without a word, he bent and scooped her up in his arms. Maggy was so startled she didn't have a chance to protest.

"Griffin, what on earth are you doing?" she asked in amusement as she wound her arms around his neck and hung on.

"Carrying you," he said simply as he strode through the

lobby of the hotel, ignoring the surprised stares and looks of the other patrons and guests.

"Yes, I can see that," Maggy whispered, snuggling closer to him and trying not to laugh. "It's not necessary though," she whispered, unbearably touched that he would risk looking ridiculous in public so she wouldn't get hurt. She'd have never believed it of him if she hadn't been here to see it for herself.

"It is necessary, Maggy," he said quietly as he nodded his thanks to the uniformed doorman who opened the lobby door for him with a generous smile. "Your shoes are tight. Your feet hurt. And I'm not about to let you walk around barefoot outdoors and perhaps hurt yourself."

The cool evening breeze slapped at them lazily. Although the temperature had cooled a bit, it was still pleasantly warm outdoors.

He shifted her higher, then made the mistake of looking at her. Her face—that beautiful mouth of hers—was a scant few inches from his and he'd resisted temptation all evening.

Now, holding Maggy in his arms again, feeling her heart beat against his, his resistance dropped like a boulder.

Telling himself he wasn't going to kiss Maggy again was like telling himself he wasn't going to breathe anymore. Impossible, he realized. Especially with her so close, and his willpower so tested.

She did something to him, something that no woman had ever done before. She made him feel things, things he'd never imagined or envisioned. Things that made him feel as if he simply couldn't get enough of her.

"Maggy." With a tilt of his head, he brushed his lips across hers, lightly at first, wanting to savor that wonderful first taste of her.

"Griffin?" Her voice was soft, breathless, while her eyes went dark with growing desire. "What…" Maggy had to swallow. Hard. It was difficult to think clearly when he was holding her, touching his lips to her, making her pulse skitter and her brain cloud. "I don't think this falls under the category of behaving professionally," she murmured against his lips, then ruined it by moaning softly and tightening her arms around him as he deepened the kiss.

He could feel her soft surrender the moment his mouth took hers fully, the soft sigh that whispered through her parted lips, the soft moan that sang in his ears.

Her arms, already around him, tightened as the world tipped, tilted then spun wildly out of control.

She ached to touch him, to feel him beneath her hands, and she slid her hand from the back of his neck to his cheek, gently, tenderly, wanting merely to touch, to soothe, to feel.

The doorman cleared his throat. Loudly. "Your car, Mr. Gibson," the man said, making Maggy and Griffin break apart guiltily.

Still flustered by her kiss, Griffin nodded his thanks, then slid into the back seat, still holding Maggy in his arms, wondering how on earth he was going to retain his sanity and get through the next month.

Dear Aunt Millie:

I'm eighty-four and my baby sister, Lulu, is seventy-nine. Last summer I met a wonderful man at church. Al is eighty-five and a longtime widower as well. Our kids are all grown, and his house and mine are paid for, but the maintenance and upkeep are getting harder and harder for us to handle. Al suggested we sell one of our houses and move in together not only to cut down on expenses, but also to cut down on the amount of required maintenance we both have to do. I think it's a great idea, but my sister is livid. She claims I'll be a fallen woman, my reputation will suffer and I'll be the scandal of the neighborhood if I live with Al without getting married. Personally, I don't give a phooey about the neighbors, nor do I want to get married—I've been married four times and these men just keep up and dying on me—but I don't want to ruin my reputation at this late stage, either. What should I do?

Old Enough in Englewood

Dear Old Enough:

Aunt Millie is certain your reputation will be quite safe. Nowadays everyone is so busy with their own lives they don't have time to worry about others. I'd say you and Al should move in together. As for Lulu, perhaps you might consider asking her to move in with you and Al as well? After all, three sharing expenses will be cheaper, and Aunt Millie has a feeling Lulu is feeling a bit left out and perhaps a tiny bit jealous of your relationship with Al. If you invite her to live with you, I'm sure she'll feel much different. Besides, you can always tell her she'll be saving your reputation.

Good luck!

Aunt Millie

Chapter Seven

"If you don't mind, dear," Millicent said to Maggy, removing her reading glasses to rub the bridge of her nose, "I'd like to quit a bit early today." She smiled. "It's Friday, so we can both get a head start on the weekend."

Maggy glanced up from her perch on the floor of Millicent's posh study, which had doubled as their joint office the past few weeks.

"Sounds like you've got weekend plans."

Millicent all but beamed. "Your grandfather and I have…well…we've decided to go away for the weekend." The words came out in a rush that caused Millicent to nearly blush. "I hope you don't mind."

"Mind?" Maggy shook her head then grinned. This was the first time in the two and half weeks since she'd been shadowing Aunt Millie that she'd ever seen Millicent flustered. It was absolutely charming, especially since she was flustered about her grandfather. "I think it's terrific,"

Maggy said, grinning wider. "Truly." Maggy got to her feet, then went over and kissed Millicent's cheek. "Where are you going?"

"I have a condo in Lake Geneva and I haven't been up there since the beginning of the summer. So I think it will be a nice change." Millicent smiled, glancing out the window where the early-fall sun filtered in, then shifted her gaze back to Maggy.

"Maggy, you've spent the past few weeks working side by side with me. You now know the routine, how we handle the incoming mail, the letters we respond to personally and publicly. You've basically learned everything that 'Aunt Millie' entails, including the numerous social and public appearances. Tell me, how do you feel about it?"

Maggy was thoughtful for a moment. "To be honest, Millicent, when I first agreed to do this—to shadow you— it was merely not to hurt your feelings or my grandfather's and so the two of you would get over the idea of me taking over your column. I really didn't think I'd be very good at this, or more importantly, very interested in it."

"And now, dear?" Millicent asked with a hopeful smile.

"Now?" Maggy was thoughtful. "During the past few weeks I've found that I really enjoy doing this." Her hand swept over the piles of letters she'd spent most of the morning sorting through. "I've come to eagerly look forward to each day's mail. For the first time in my life I feel like I'm making a difference, actually doing something that's important."

Millicent laughed. "That can be a very addictive feeling."

"Yes, it can," Maggy agreed with a smile. She frowned suddenly. "I can't say I'm as delighted with all the social engagements, but they're bearable, for now at least."

"Well," Millicent said carefully, "I'm trying not to get

my hopes up, and since I asked for a month and we've still got one and a half more weeks to go until the month is up, I won't press you for an answer now, but I'm hoping that you will see that you were meant to do this." Millicent hesitated. "I watched you, worked with you every single day, listened to your advice, observed how you relate to people, and I've never seen anyone better. I do think this is your true calling."

Maggy was grateful she wasn't going to be pushed for a decision now since she still hadn't made up her mind. "Thanks, Millicent. I appreciate your confidence, and the opportunity you've given me. Regardless of my final decision, I want you to know how much I appreciate what you've done for me."

"You're welcome. No one has been more deserving." Crossing her legs, Millicent sat back. "Now, dear, what on earth are we going to do about my stuffy, suspicious grandson?"

"I'm coming, I'm coming," Maggy called, hurrying through the apartment Friday evening as someone knocked again. Through the glass in the door, Maggy could see Griffin, dressed as usual in one of his spiffy, three-piece suits in spite of the fact that it was after six on a Friday evening.

Didn't the man ever relax? she wondered. Or had he been born in that suit?

Although she felt an instant of delight and distress at the sight of him, she glanced down at herself and wanted to groan. The moment she'd gotten home from Millicent's she'd kicked off her shoes, changed into one of her oldest, most comfortable pair of shorts and one of her brothers' old T-shirts.

"Griffin." Self-conscious because of her appearance, she pulled open the door with a smile. "Hi. Come on in." From the look on his face, her pulse jittered nervously. "Oh my God, did I forget some social thingy that was scheduled for tonight?"

She was pretty sure she had everything marked in the daily planner he'd bought her and insisted she use. She detested having a schedule of her time and had lost the first two planners he'd purchased. Now she was on number three, and determined not to lose it. But at the moment, she couldn't quite remember where it was or what exactly was in it.

"No," he said with a smile. "We don't have anything on the schedule until Tuesday." He held something up in the air. "But you left your compact in the limo last night and Ernie thought you might need it." He handed the small black compact to her. Their fingers brushed and Griffin sighed. He had hoped that during the past few weeks his body would get used to Maggy, get used to her and simply stop responding to her like a randy teenager. Unfortunately, it had never happened. In fact, if anything, his reaction to her had simply gotten stronger.

He found himself thinking of her at odd times throughout the day and at night. The nights were much harder. He lay awake staring at his bedroom ceiling, unable to chase Maggy from his mind.

He found himself looking forward to seeing her, to being with her, and kept trying to find silly excuses to see her when they didn't have a social engagement scheduled. He'd even taken to driving past her house, hoping for a glimpse of her.

He'd been at a loss today, though, fearing he had no reason to see her through the weekend, and knowing he wouldn't be able to rest or relax if he had to go two long days without seeing her. It would, he realized, drive him mad. He'd hoped to perhaps take her to dinner tonight, or to one of the new jazz clubs that had opened downtown.

"Would you like something to drink?" Maggy asked politely, crossing one bare foot over the other self-consciously. "Perhaps a glass of wine?"

"Got a beer?" he asked with a grin, pulling out a chair and sitting down.

She merely stared at him. "A beer? You want a beer?" she repeated.

"Yeah, something wrong with that?"

She chuckled. "No, not at all," she said, going to the refrigerator and pulling it open to extract a cold beer. "But I hardly pictured you as the beer-drinking type." In all the social engagements they'd attended, he usually drank wine, or once in a while, usually at the end of the evening, a straight Irish whiskey. He'd never had a beer that she knew of.

"Why?" he asked, shaking his head at the glass she offered and tipping the bottle to his lips for a quick sip. "I drank beer all through college." He laughed. "It was all I could afford."

"I doubt that," she said, realizing with the kind of family money he had, Griffin could probably have afforded his own brewery if he wanted.

"It's awfully quiet around here tonight," Griffin said.

"My grandfather went away for the weekend so I'm alone." Maggy retrieved a cold soft drink for herself and joined him at the kitchen table. "My brother Michael was supposed to stop by tonight, but he called, he's back on another undercover assignment, so I thought I'd just stay in and get a pizza." She hesitated for a moment. "Would you like to join me?"

He glanced at her, then grinned. Suddenly pizza with

Maggy sounded more appealing than the finest dinner or show. "If you throw in a couple of movies, preferably *Creature Features,* you've got yourself a deal."

Her smile flashed at the idea of spending the evening with him doing something as simple and relaxing as having a pizza and watching movies. It was her idea of a perfect evening. "Really?"

"Really." He stripped off his jacket, hanging it over the back of the chair, then loosened his tie, slipping it over his head and dropping it over his jacket.

"How on earth can you stand to wear that thing wrapped around your neck all day?" she asked with a scowl.

He laughed. "I can't, but you get used to it."

"I don't think so," she said. "Come on, let's go into the living room."

"Your grandfather went away for the weekend?" he said after sinking into the comfortable but well-worn couch, hoping Maggy was going to sit next to him. "That's funny, so did my grandmother."

Maggy smiled, sitting next to him and setting down her soda on the table in front of the couch. "I know. They went away together." The look that crossed his face would have been comical had she not had the earlier conversation with his grandmother.

"Together?" Griffin asked through narrowed eyes, leaning forward as his body tensed. "What do you mean *together?*"

Maggy wanted to sigh. She recognized that tone of voice by now. It was his highly displeased, suspicious tone and it never failed to raise her hackles.

"Well, your grandmother and my grandfather have gone to Lake Geneva to spend the weekend together." One eyebrow rose as she sensed his displeasure. "Is that clearer?"

"Very. But why?" he asked with a shake of his head.

"Why what?" Maggy asked. She'd always thought this living room more than big enough, but with just her and Griffin in it, it suddenly seemed far too small.

"Why on earth would they go away together?" Griffin asked with a frown. He'd been spending so much time with Maggy, he hadn't really been keeping as close an eye on Patrick as he would have liked or clearly he would have known about this before now.

"Griffin," Maggy began carefully, struggling not to laugh. "Haven't you ever gone away for the weekend with a woman?"

"Well, of course I have, but that's different," he said stiffly, feeling slightly defensive.

"And exactly why is that different?" Maggy demanded, eyes flashing as her temper began to stir.

He drew back. "You can't be serious."

"I'm totally serious. Now what's different about them going away together as opposed to you and a woman?"

"Maggy, please, let's be reasonable here."

"Excuse me, Griffin, but I don't think I'm the one being unreasonable." She cocked her head to look at him. "Are you blind, or hasn't it occurred to you that they may be in love with each other?"

"In love?" he almost scoffed, then saw the look on her face. "At their age don't you think that's a bit ludicrous?" He would have laughed except for the look on her face.

"What on earth is ludicrous about it?" she demanded, her voice rising. "Love isn't bound by any boundaries. It can happen anytime, anywhere, to anyone, regardless of age. And if they're lucky enough to find love, at any age, but especially at their age, I think they should go for it." She studied his face for a moment. "You don't agree?"

Griffin shook his head, his brain muddled from Maggy's nearness and this entire conversation.

Dusk was just settling in, casting deep amber shadows across the room from the large living-room windows, bathing Maggy in a soft, ethereal glow. She'd never looked more beautiful.

Trying to get his mind back on the problem at hand, he shifted his gaze away from her, not wanting to be distracted again. They'd been talking about his grandmother and her grandfather, and Griffin scowled, realizing they were away together and alone for the entire weekend.

"Love is something that's far too complicated for me to even try to figure out," Griffin said, holding his hands in the air. "I'm not going to touch that one."

"Are you saying you don't believe in love?" Maggy asked, truly shocked.

Sensing he was on dangerous ground, Griffin shook his head. "No, Maggy, I'm sorry, I don't believe in love," he admitted without a trace of guilt or sadness. "I don't believe in anything that has its basis in emotion. Emotions can change like the wind, or shifting sand, and aren't very stable at the best of times. To believe in love, to believe it can last a lifetime or even a long time—well, I'm sorry but my practical mind tells me that's a foolish thing to believe in. There's usually something else at stake," he said, thinking of his own dismal experiences as well as his father's numerous escapades with women. "Something else someone wants."

His words about love made a strong, sharp ache in the center in her heart. She'd never before met anyone who didn't believe in love. It was so unbearably sad she couldn't help but feel sorry for Griffin, and wonder what had hurt him so badly to make him so cynical. And then she remembered what he'd told her about his father. No wonder the man felt there was no such thing as love with the parental example he'd had.

Maggy huffed out a sigh. She had a feeling they were back on familiar ground again. "And you think my grandfather's after your grandmother's money, as opposed to her heart, right?" It hurt, she realized, hurt that Griffin didn't believe in love, and hurt that he could think so little of her grandfather, especially now that he'd had a chance to get to know him the past few weeks. Annoyed and disappointed, Maggy shook her head. "How can you have so little faith in your grandmother?" she wondered aloud. "How can you just assume money is the only thing she has to offer someone?" The thought simply appalled her.

Her words gave him pause. He never really thought of it that way, as if the only reason someone would love his grandmother was for her money. That certainly wasn't the case, nor what he believed. His grandmother was the most wonderful, intelligent woman he'd ever met.

"It's not that I think that's all she has to offer someone," Griffin began carefully. "On the contrary, she has quite a bit to offer someone."

"But nothing as important as her money," Maggy finished for him.

"Maggy," he began carefully. "You have to understand. From my experience—"

"With your father," she inserted carefully, and he nodded. Once again she could see the pain in his face and it nearly broke her heart to know that Griffin had never had all the things she'd always had and took for granted. Family love, total and unconditional.

"Yes, with my father, and again with my own experience with women."

"Are you saying women only date you for your money?" Now she really was shocked. He was gorgeous, intelligent and great fun to be around—when he wasn't being cynical and suspicious.

"It's been known to happen," he admitted, thinking of Marissa.

"Then I'm sorry for you, Griffin. I imagine knowing someone wants you for something as unimportant as money or material goods is pretty insulting not to mention hurtful." She laughed suddenly. "I wish I could say I understand, but I don't since I've never had any kind of money to speak of and am still struggling to put myself through school."

Griffin frowned. "But if your grandfather truly has his own money, Maggy, why wouldn't he help you?"

She smiled, taking a sip of her soft drink and settling herself more comfortably on the couch. "He would," she said. "But I won't take any money from him. That's his money. Not mine. I work for what I want, Griffin." She shrugged. "It's always been that way. All of us, including my brothers, we've all worked since high school. We'd never dream of letting someone else pay our way." She hesitated, wondering if he could understand this. "I think it has something to do with pride and independence. If you have to work hard for something you truly want, then when you get it, you truly appreciate it because you have had to work so hard for it."

"That makes sense," he agreed, then smiled, touching the ends of her hair with the tips of his fingers. It flashed like fire, and was just as silky as he'd remembered. "I worked my way through college," he said. "That's how I learned to enjoy beer." Chuckling, he held up his bottle. "It was all I could afford."

"Griffin, why did you work your way through college?" This sounded implausible considering the family wealth he came from.

"Well, like you, I wouldn't take money from my grandparents. Although I received a full scholarship to the University of Arizona, I worked all four years for spending money, books and the likes."

"Griffin," she began carefully, wondering if she was about to tread into a minefield. "What about your father? Didn't he help you?"

He shook his head, and that same painful expression settled on his features. "No," he said flatly. "My father hasn't contributed one penny to my support since the day he left us."

Maggy nearly shuddered at the cold, detached way he said it, as if he were speaking of someone else. "Griffin, how long has it been since you've seen your father?" From what little he'd told her about his father, she knew his relationship with him was still estranged.

Thinking, Griffin hesitated for a moment, sipping his beer. "He moved to California shortly after he left us so it's been more than twenty years."

"Surely you've seen him sometime since then."

"Well, yes and no." He went on at the confusion on her face. "Right before I left for college, since I was going to be living one state away in Arizona, I thought it was time to try to establish some kind of connection with him." Griffin shook his head. "I thought I'd matured enough to perhaps forgive him for what he'd done to us." He hesitated. "For a long time, I blamed him for my mother's death. Somehow in my youthful mind I believed she wouldn't have gotten sick, wouldn't have died if he'd been there." He shook his head then took a sip of beer to wash away the bitterness in his mouth. He had to take a deep breath before continuing, surprised to find he was a bit shaky. "Anyway, I called him one day about a month before leaving for the University of Arizona. I had to fly to Tucson for orientation, and thought I'd spend the weekend with him." He chuckled, but there was no humor in the sound. "I told him I was coming to Los Angeles for the weekend to see him."

"And was he pleased?" Maggy asked hopefully.

Griffin turned to her. "I don't know since I never had a chance to see him."

"What happened?" she asked softly, covering his hand with hers, needing to comfort him.

"He had his driver pick me up from the airport—"

"Wait a minute," Maggy said with a shake of her head. "You hadn't seen or heard from your father in over ten years then, except for his wedding announcements and he didn't bother to pick you up himself?"

"Uh…no, Maggy. As he told me, he was a very busy man." He sighed, then glanced down at his beer. "He'd just remarried again." He lifted his gaze to hers and she could see the remnants of sadness. "A young model, and he was trying to negotiate a new contract for her. Anyway, his driver took me to a hotel. A very nice hotel," he clarified, patting her hand when she scowled. "We were scheduled to have dinner that night, but he never showed up at the restaurant. I waited two hours, but apparently he got 'tied up' as he explained in his phone message later."

"Didn't he even try to see you?" she asked, wondering what kind of man his father was. How could he go so many years without seeing his son, and then just ignore him when he specifically went to visit him.

"No, he didn't, Maggy." At the look on her face, he lifted her hand and kissed it. "Don't look so furious and shocked. Leopards don't change their spots no matter how many years pass." He shrugged his shoulders as if easily dismissing his father's neglect, but she knew it couldn't be that simple or that easy. "As he reminded me. He was a very busy man and I certainly couldn't expect him to drop everything simply to cater to my whims, as he put it."

"Whims," she repeated through clenched teeth, desperately trying to hold her tongue and her temper. "What did you do?" she asked softly, aware that he'd linked his fingers with hers and was holding on tightly to her hand. She wondered if he realized how tense he became every time he spoke of his father. But considering what the man had put him through, it was easy to understand why. No wonder Griffin was so cynical and suspicious. With his experiences it wasn't hard to understand.

"I went back to the hotel, packed my bags and took a cab to the airport." He turned to look at her. "I flew to Tucson that night, went to orientation and put the whole thing behind me. I've never heard from him again."

"Oh, Griffin, I'm so sorry." She rested her forehead against his, her heart aching for him. His enticing scent was wreaking havoc with her control. Never in her life had she wanted to comfort anyone more. Her own heart literally hurt from the pain of his father's rejection. She had no idea how anyone could treat their own child that way. "So very sorry. The man ought to be shot."

Shaking his head and feeling embarrassed that he'd opened up to Maggy and told her things he'd never discussed with anyone, not even his grandmother, Griffin tried to rein in some control. "I'm afraid it would be a waste of a perfectly good bullet." He forced a smile and set down his beer. "You know, Maggy, not everyone is cut out to be a father. Some people just don't have the temperament or the personality to be a parent. I think my dad is one of them."

"Did he ever have any more children?"

Griffin shook his head. "I'm not sure, but I really don't think so." He blew out a breath, anxious to get off the subject of his father. He tried not to think or talk about the man simply because it was nothing more than an exercise in futility. "Enough about my father," he said, blowing out a breath as if he could simply blow away the painful experience. When he turned to her, he managed a small smile. "Why don't you order our pizza and I'll run out and get the movies."

"Terrific." Maggy smiled, taking a steadying breath and trying to get her temper back under control. "There's a video store right around the corner, next door to the funeral parlor. Just tell Max, he'll be the old man behind the counter, that the movies are for Maggy."

One eyebrow lifted. "And this Max, he's just going to hand over some movies to me, a perfect stranger?"

She laughed. "Of course. Max knows everyone in the neighborhood, and their tastes. He'll have something we should both enjoy."

Griffin stood up and drained his beer. "Okay," he said skeptically. "But I've never rented movies from a new store without having to produce identification, a credit card and enough proof of who I am to get me into a foreign country."

Laughing, Maggy stood as well. "Well, then, it's clear you haven't been renting at the right places. Just tell Max you're a friend of mine."

"And you expect Max to just believe me?"

"Why wouldn't he?"

Shaking his head in disbelief, Griffin smiled. "Okay, I'll try it, but no guarantees."

"A large cheese and sausage pizza?" she asked, and he nodded.

"With extra cheese," they both said at almost the same time. Laughing, Griffin headed into the kitchen to grab his jacket.

"I'll be right back," he said over his shoulder, realizing he hadn't been looking forward to an evening the way he was looking forward to tonight in a long, long time. But then again, he realized, just being with Maggy seemed to make everything special. It should have worried him, but he realized suddenly, it didn't.

At midnight, Griffin stifled a yawn just as the ending credits of the last movie began to roll. He couldn't remember when he'd had a more relaxing evening.

"Maggy, I almost forgot. Do you have plans tomorrow?" he asked, glancing down at her. She was snuggled against him, her head on his shoulder, his arm around her. Her hair smelled like roses, he decided, fresh, fragrant roses, and was as soft and silky as the most delicate petals.

"Plans?" Stifling a yawn of her own, Maggy's groggy mind went into overdrive as she sat up, straightening her T-shirt. School started in less than three weeks and she'd yet to register for her classes, buy her books or anything else. "I was planning on going to register for school, but if you need me for something, I can postpone it."

"No," he said quickly. "It's nothing official or anything like that. It's more…personal," he said, feeling a bit uncomfortable. Other than tonight, he'd never officially asked her to go out or asked her to do anything with him that wasn't an official "Aunt Millie" social engagement. "I was just wondering if you'd like to go fishing."

Her eyebrows rose. "Fishing?" She shook her head,

stunned. If he'd asked her to go Irish step dancing naked down Michigan Avenue she wouldn't have been more shocked. "You like to fish?" The man was full of surprises, she decided.

He grinned and sat up, rubbing his shoulder a bit. It had grown stiff being in one position so long. But he liked the feel of Maggy so close, their bodies connecting and touching, he hadn't wanted to move. "I don't know since I've never been fishing before."

"But you've decided to take up fishing now?" she asked, realizing there was clearly more to this than he was saying. She wished the man would just open up and speak and not make her pull information from him like a reluctant confessor.

"Yes and no."

"Well, that clarifies it, then," she said with a nod and a sleepy smile.

"You know Ernie, your driver?" When she nodded, he went on. "Well, he's got an eight-year-old grandson he hasn't seen in a couple of years. Ernie and his daughter apparently don't get along very well, and she wouldn't let Ernie see his grandson."

"I know, we talked about it a couple of weeks ago. Ernie is crazy about his grandson, but I can't even imagine a daughter being so coldhearted toward her own father." Remembering the conversation they had about Griffin's father earlier in the evening, Maggy immediately regretted her words, realizing not everyone was privileged enough to have a warm, loving family as she'd had.

"I know. I think it's appalling as well, so I promised Ernie when I hired him that I'd try to get him some grandparent visitation rights. Before actually going to court, I decided to try talking to his daughter myself, to see if I could reason with her. So I went to see her yesterday. I told her Ernie was now working for me, living in the YMCA and would have his own apartment in a couple of weeks. He's become a fully functioning member of society again, and I don't see any reason for him not to be allowed to spend time with his grandson." Griffin shrugged as her eyes misted. "It's not that big of a deal, Maggy."

"Yes, Griffin," she said, laying a hand to his cheek and feeling her heart all but melt. "It's a very big deal. To Ernie and I'm sure to his grandson." She hesitated, remembering her conversation with Ernie earlier in the month. "That boy means a great deal to Ernie."

"I know." Griffin frowned. "He's the apple of Ernie's eye, so I figured if I talked to his daughter, maybe she'd reconsider and let Ernie see the kid."

"And did she? Reconsider?"

Griffin smiled, a full blown smile that had Maggy's nerves squealing. "Yep. We had a nice long chat. I can't say she's totally thrilled about the idea, but since I promised to chaperon Ernie and her son—provided she let Ernie take him out for the day—she finally agreed to let Ernie see the boy twice a month."

Maggy laughed, knowing how formidable Griffin could be when he set his mind to something. "So you're going fishing with them?"

"That's the plan." Griffin rubbed his jaw where the end-of-the-day stubble was forming.

For a man who had no experience with fathers or families, he was certainly going out of his way to ensure that Ernie had a chance to get to see his own grandson and be part of his life.

Griffin's kindness to others so touched her heart, Maggy wanted to grab him up in a hug and just hold him. To give him all the love, caring and tenderness he'd missed out on as a child from his father. And, judging from his comments, had missed out on as an adult simply because he had such a hard time believing in love, people or trust. And she realized that was the essence of Griffin's concern about her grandfather's intentions—it was simply a matter of letting go and believing in someone and trusting them.

"You're giving up your own time so Ernie can see his grandson?"

Griffin shrugged, trying to ignore the softening in her eyes, the sweetness of her mouth.

"Tell me something," she asked carefully. "Why did you do this? I mean, what made you decide to help Ernie?"

He shrugged. "Why not? I don't think money or status should be a ruling factor when it comes to parenting or grandparenting. Just because Ernie lost his job and his apartment doesn't necessarily make him a bad grandparent or a bad influence. Anyone can have hard times or a spot of bad luck, I don't think they should lose their family over it.

"Maggy, I don't know what I would have done after my mother's death if my grandparents hadn't taken me in and raised me." He hesitated a moment, glancing down at his hands. "My grandfather meant the world to me. We were very close, probably closer than most sons and fathers, and certainly closer than I ever was to my own father. My relationship with my grandfather helped define who I am and what I'm all about." His gaze softened at the mention of his grandfather. "My grandfather was the finest man I've ever known. He was kind, loving, considerate and the most honorable man I've ever met. From him I learned what it means to be a man, to accept and handle responsibility. He taught me more than I can ever say."

"You still miss him?" Maggy said softly, her own heart

aching for Griffin and his loss. Her grandfather meant so much to her, she had no idea what she'd do without him. She couldn't even bear to think of it.

"Every day of my life," he admitted. "Even though he's been gone several years now, I still find myself picking up the phone to call him, to just ask his advice or discuss a tough case." Griffin smiled at his own foolishness. "He was so much a part of my life that it's hard to get used to life without him." He glanced down for a moment before glancing back up at her. "I just thought he'd be here forever," he said softly, an unusual ache in his voice. Trying to banish the feelings, Griffin rubbed a hand over his face, trying to get himself back on track. Emotions always scared him, especially his own. "But I guess we always think the people we love, the people who are the most important to us, will always be here for us, and that's not usually the case," he finished quietly.

She was watching him intently. Her hair was slightly mussed, her eyes a bit sleepy, and Griffin realized at that moment, like his grandfather, he'd gotten so used to having Maggy in his life, he couldn't imagine his day-to-day life without her.

Then it struck him like a knife to his heart. Maggy *wouldn't* always be around. She'd agreed to shadow his grandmother for a month. At the time she'd agreed, a month seemed like an eternity.

Now that he'd gotten to know Maggy, a month didn't nearly seem long enough.

And it worried and troubled him. He could almost feel the loss of Maggy in his life already and knew it wasn't something he was looking forward to.

Griffin reached for her hand again, holding on tightly as if he could simply hold her in his life forever.

But he knew that was impossible. At the end of the month, Maggy would go her way, and he would go his, back to his old life before Maggy. Funny, right now he couldn't even seem to remember what his life was like without her.

Boring, his mind whispered. Boring and lonely.

"So you're going to take the boy fishing?"

"Yep, and I just thought maybe you'd like to join us."

Maggy grinned, thrilled that he'd thought to include her and excited that she'd get to spend the whole day with Griffin. They'd never actually done anything that wasn't in some related to "Aunt Millie." Until now. "I'd love to," she said, meaning it.

"What about your classes, though?" he asked with a frown. "I don't want to interfere with your schedule."

"No, it's all right. I can register next week." She touched his arm. "Really, Griffin. I'd much rather go fishing with you and Ernie than spend the day standing in line waiting to register for classes that will no doubt already be full."

"You're sure?" His gaze searched hers and he felt that inexplicable pull again, the one that made his heart ache and his hands itch to touch her. Just to touch her. It was becoming a habit, this need to touch Maggy, to be with her, to see her.

"I'm positive, Griffin." She flashed him a brilliant smile, touching the back of his hand. "Absolutely positive. Besides, I haven't been fishing all summer, and it will be nice to get some time in before the cooler weather sets in." Self-conscious because of the way Griffin was looking at her, Maggy ran a hand through her hair, knowing it probably looked a sight after having her head on Griffin's shoulder for so many hours.

"Great." Knowing she'd be joining them, and he would

get to spend the whole day with her again, immediately lifted Griffin's spirits, but he frowned suddenly. "We planned on leaving early, but I've got to hit the store first since I don't have one piece of fishing equipment, and Ernie said he lost all of his when he was evicted from his apartment."

"Don't worry about it. We've got the entire Gallagher family store of fishing equipment down in the basement, everything from poles to lures."

"Lures?" Griffin repeated dully, making Maggy laugh.

"I see we're going to have to include a crash course in Fishing 101 for you as well."

Stifling another yawn, Griffin stood up, taking Maggy's hand and pulling her up with him. "That might be a good idea since I don't know one end of a fishing pole from another."

Standing so close to him, she could smell his masculine scent, feel the warmth of his body drawing her closer. She had to order herself to remain still and to stop being jumpy. But Griffin's nearness always did that to her. Made every nerve jerk awake as if from a long, deep sleep.

"How about we pick you up about ten?" he asked, his gaze intent on hers.

"Terrific." She lifted a hand and brushed a stray strand of hair off his forehead, giving in to the need and desire to touch him. "I'll pack a picnic lunch for us." Her eyebrows drew together for a moment. "Do you have any idea where you want to go fishing?"

"Where?" Griffin swallowed hard. "No, not really. I figured Ernie would know a place."

"Well, don't worry about it. If he doesn't, we have a small cabin right on Fox Lake. It's kind of primitive, but it should do the trick. And the fishing up there is spectacular. My dad used to take us there every summer."

"Good." Shifting nervously, Griffin slid his hands in his pockets. Maggy was too close to him, too close to resist, and he knew if he didn't get out of here, didn't keep his hands to himself, he'd be reaching for her again. "Thank you for tonight, Maggy. I can't remember when I've had a more enjoyable evening."

She smiled. He was so formal and polite it always tickled her to no end. Just once she wished he'd let his hair down and relax and let himself go.

"You're welcome, I appreciate the company. With Grandpa gone, and all my brothers working or out on dates, I would have spent the evening alone if you hadn't come by."

"Well, I guess I'd better get going then," he said without making a move to leave.

"Yeah, I guess so." She looked up at him, let her gaze travel over that beautiful face of his, felt something strong and fierce pull at her heart. Instinct had her taking a step closer to him until her bare toes were almost touching the elegant tips of his shoes. "Griffin?" The word was a soft, sweet question as she stood on tiptoe and gently brushed her lips across his.

He stood there for a moment, trying to hang on to his sanity and his control.

He was certain he was losing both.

He found his hands sliding free of his pockets to reach for her, pulling her close until the entire length of her body was pressed against his, and he exhaled a sigh of deep relief, as if holding her in his arms filled and completed him in a way that he never even knew he needed or missed. Until now. Until Maggy.

"Maggy." He simply said her name, it was all he could manage as the hands at her waist drew her closer, savoring the soft sweetness of her mouth, her taste.

Lifting her hands to his chest, Maggy sighed in pleaure, allowing herself to revel in the feelings that began stampeding through her the moment Griffin touched her, kissed her.

They hadn't bothered to light any lamps, merely a few candles that now flickered in the surrounding darkness, enclosing them in a quiet romantic cocoon.

Aware of his own needs, and knowing they were all alone in the house, Griffin knew he had to keep a tight rein on his control.

With deep regret, he ended the kiss, letting his lips gently brush against hers softly, once, twice and then finally a third time before pulling away, knowing if he didn't, in a few minutes he might not be able to.

"Thanks again," he said softly, taking her hand. "Come on, walk me to the door so you can lock up before I leave."

Shaking her head with a laugh, Maggy followed him, allowing him to lead her through the house to the back door in the kitchen. Only Griffin would be worried about her safety in her own neighborhood. It was so sweet and caring, she didn't have the heart to tell him she not only knew everyone in the neighborhood, but with three brothers who were cops the chances of anyone picking her or her house to victimize was remote at best. All she had to do was toss open a window and scream and everyone from Mr. Murphy the undertaker to Al the barber would be at her house in a flash—along with all her brothers and probably three-quarters of the police force.

Still, it touched her to know he was concerned about her and her safety.

"I'll see you at ten, then?" Griffin said as she opened the door for him.

"Ten it is." She opened the door wider, leaning against

it to watch him through eyes that were dreamy and a little sleepy. "Oh, and Griffin, you might want to think of something else to wear." She had to bank a smile when he glanced down at himself. "A three-piece suit and Italian shoes are probably not the best getup for fishing."

"What are you wearing?" he asked with a smile, making her glance down at herself.

"Pretty much something similar to what I've got on. So if you've got a pair of cutoffs and an old shirt, that would be perfect. Oh, and if you've got any bathing trunks, bring those along as well."

"Swimming? You expect me to go swimming?"

"Well, it's still warm enough and I'm betting the water will be, too." Cocking her head, she looked at him carefully. "Don't tell me you've never been swimming."

"Not anywhere but a heated pool, but there's a first time for everything." He leaned forward and kissed her on the forehead. "I'll see you in the morning." He walked out the door. "Now, close and lock the door when I leave."

"Yes, sir," she said with a mock salute, shutting the door and turning the locks and dead bolt so he could hear it. She pushed the window curtain aside and waved to him.

"Good night, Griffin," she mouthed, and he nodded before heading down the stairs.

With a sigh, Maggy leaned against the door, stifling another yawn, wondering how Griffin-who-didn't-believe-in-love would feel if he knew she was falling in love with him.

Dear Aunt Millie:

My mother-in-law tends to be a bit pushy and bossy. She gave us a gift certificate for a very nice store for our anniversary. When she asked what I was going to use it for, I told her I wanted to get a new set of dishes, which I did. Last week, she stayed with our children while I accompanied my husband on a business trip. When we returned, I learned my mother-in-law had returned the dishes I'd bought with the gift certificate for a pattern that she liked better. Needless to say, I was not only stunned, but hurt since I liked the pattern I chose. I don't want to seem ungrateful, but I hate the dishes she picked out and feel resentment every time I have to use them. What should I do?

Betrayed in Bensenville

Dear Betrayed:

I would take the dishes back and get the ones you want. Explain to your mother-in-law that since she gave you a choice by giving you a gift certificate, you and your husband choose the pattern you liked. If she prefers the other pattern, tell her you'll be happy to return the favor and give her a gift certificate for her anniversary so she can get the dishes she likes.

Good luck!

Aunt Millie

Chapter Eight

"Mr. Gibson?" Sitting on the edge of the pier that soared out and over Fox Lake, eight-year-old Sammy tried to mimic Griffin who had his feet in the water, swaying them to and fro. Too small to reach, Sammy kept scooting closer and closer to the edge of the pier, making Griffin nervous. "Do you like your big black car that you let my grandpa drive?" Sammy turned to Griffin, squinting against the bright afternoon sunlight.

Griffin smiled, reaching over to help the boy steady his fishing pole. They'd been sitting on the pier for almost four hours, taking a soft-drink break now and again and checking their lures and poles more frequently than that. Sammy and Maggy, who was sitting across from them on the opposite side of the pier, close enough to hear their conversation but far enough away to enjoy her own fishing spot, had caught the most fish so far, leaving him and poor Ernie in the dust.

"Yes, I like it, Sammy," Griffin said. "But it's not my car, it's just leased."

Sammy frowned. "I don't know what that means," he admitted, wiping his sweaty nose with the back of his hand.

Griffin's eyes twinkled. While he'd never had much experience with children, he found himself totally enchanted with Sammy, who had a curious mind and a question about almost anything that caught his fancy. "It means that the car belongs to someone else and I just pay them to let me use it."

"And then you pay my grandpa to drive it, right?"

Griffin nodded. "That's right."

"Mr. Gibson?" Fidgeting his butt on the old wooden pier, Sammy inched closer to the edge of the pier.

"Yes?" Griffin reached out a hand and hauled the boy back and away from the water. "Don't forget what I said, Sammy. Don't get too close. That water is very deep." And he wasn't certain his swimming skills were up to rescuing anyone.

"Do you think my grandpa could take me for a ride in the big black car sometime?" Sammy's eyebrows drew together. "I've never been in a car with my grandpa before."

Griffin turned and pulled the boy's billed Chicago Cubs baseball cap lower on his face to try to protect his nose from the glare and heat of the sun. "I don't see why not."

"Does that mean yes?" Sammy asked.

Griffin laughed. "Yes, it does."

"Mr. Gibson?"

"Yes, son?"

"Don't you got enough money to buy your own car?"

Griffin laughed, then shook his head. "I suppose I could buy my own car if I wanted."

"Then why don'tcha?" Sammy asked with a deep frown. "Buy your own car?"

"Boy, when you gonna stop bothering Mr. Gibson with all those questions?" Ernie asked with a smile, turning to his grandson.

"It's all right, Ernie," Griffin said, turning to smile at Maggy and Ernie. "I don't mind." He turned back to Sammy. "Actually, Sammy, I kind of like having your grandpa drive me around. He's a very good driver."

"I know." Sammy nodded, then turned and beamed a grin at his grandpa before turning back to Griffin. "My mom has her own car, but she won't let no one else drive it. Not even Grandpa." Sammy blew a bubble from the gum Maggy had given him earlier. "Do you got a dog?" His bubble popped big, pink and loud, making him and Maggy grin.

"A dog?" Griffin shook his head, glancing out over the water at the sun, which was slowly sinking toward the horizon. He hated to see this day end. It had been wonderful and totally relaxing, much to his surprise. "Nope. No dog. Dogs aren't allowed in my building."

"Well, do you got a wife, then?" Sammy asked with a frown, clearly not liking the answers he'd been getting.

Griffin hesitated for a moment, glancing over his shoulder at Maggy, who was simply looking at him curiously, waiting to hear his answer. He wished she didn't look quite so tickled about this line of questioning. "No, no wife, either."

"Do you got any kids?"

Griffin sighed. "Nope, no kids, either, Sammy. Sorry."

"Are you a loser, Mr. Gibson?"

"Sammy!" Ernie was standing up now, looming over his grandson, mortally embarrassed. "Why on earth would you ask the man something like that?"

Sammy shrugged his slender shoulders. "Mama says

that if you don't got a car, or a dog or a wife, and if you don't got no kids, then you're a loser."

"Come here, Sammy," Maggy said, turning and sliding over next to where Griffin was sitting. She held her arms out to Sammy, who handed Griffin his fishing pole, then all but climbed into Maggy's lap, settling himself comfortably.

"Sweetheart," Maggy began, aware that her bare legs were brushing right up against Griffin's bare legs now. The man had actually worn a pair of khaki shorts and a polo shirt, surprising her by looking totally sexy in his casual wear and making her heart pound simply by his nearness. "Just because someone doesn't own a car or a dog, or have a wife or kids it doesn't mean he's a loser."

"But that's what my mama said," Sammy reminded her with a frown. Maggy glanced helplessly at Ernie, who was still looming over them, his face a mask of shock, shaking his head, clearly disappointed in his daughter.

"Sammy." After handing Maggy his fishing pole, Griffin reached for the boy, pulling him from Maggy's lap into his. "I want you to listen to me, okay?" He waited for the boy to nod solemnly. "Sometimes people say things they don't mean. And sometimes people think that things are important."

"Things?" Sammy repeated with a scowl, swiping the back of his hand against his sweaty nose again and clearly not understanding.

"Yes, like cars or bikes or houses or toys—"

"You mean stuff," Sammy said with a grin, suddenly understanding.

"Yeah, stuff," Griffin said, pleased he was finally speaking the boy's language. "But stuff is not really important and not having stuff doesn't make you a loser."

"It doesn't?" Sammy asked, wide-eyed, and Griffin shook his head.

"No, it doesn't, Sammy." Griffin glanced up at Ernie, then back at the boy. "Let me tell you something, Sammy. My own grandpa—"

"You got a grandpa?" Sammy said in awe. "But you're old," Sammy announced with a scowl, making them all laugh.

"Yes, well." Griffin cleared his throat. "Even though I'm old, Sammy. I wasn't always so old." He flashed a look at Maggy who was desperately trying not to grin. "Anyway, when I was growing up, spending time with my grandpa was the most important thing in the world to me. Even more important than a dog, or a car, or anything else for that matter." Griffin glanced at Ernie. "Now, Sammy, your grandpa here, well, you're very lucky to have him in your life. He loves you very much, and spending time with you is very important to him, more important than anything else in the world." Griffin met the boy's solemn gaze. "Wouldn't you rather be able to see your grandpa, spend time with him—"

"And go fishing with him?" Sammy inserted with a wide grin, making Griffin smile and nod.

"Yes, and go fishing with him. Wouldn't you rather do those things than have a toy or other stuff?"

"Yeah, but that's cuz I love my grandpa," Sammy said, crossing his arms across his skinny chest and making Ernie beam proudly.

"And he loves you, too, Sammy," Griffin explained patiently. "Just like my grandpa loved me. So you see, son, stuff isn't nearly as important as having someone you love in your life." Griffin hesitated, glancing at Maggy for reassurance, relieved when she gave him a silent nod, her eyes shining with unshed tears. Until this moment, he'd never realized the importance of his statement. Until he met Maggy, he'd never realized, never even considered love important or integral to his own life. "Having people who love you in your life is far more important than all the things and stuff in the world. Do you understand what I mean?"

"I think so," Sammy said slowly, then grinned hugely, revealing one missing front tooth. "But does that mean I can't have a dog if I got a grandpa?"

"Today was certainly an education," Griffin said with a moan as he climbed the back steps to Maggy's apartment and rubbed his aching stomach. Dusk had settled almost into full darkness, and the moon hung high and bright in the blackened sky. "I cannot believe how much pizza that child ate."

Maggy laughed. "He's a growing boy. Wait until he hits his teens, it gets worse."

Griffin all but shuddered. "I'm glad I don't have to pay his food bill."

"Be glad you didn't have to pay to feed six growing boys." Reaching the top of the stairs, Maggy stifled a yawn, then leaned against the closed back door. "It's a good thing Grandpa owned a deli or he would have ended up in the poorhouse considering the way my brothers ate."

"I can well imagine." Griffin reached out and touched the silky tips of her hair. "Thanks for coming with us today, Maggy. I really appreciated it, along with all the tips on fishing." He smiled at her, totally relaxed and comfortable. "Even though I only caught two fish, I'd have to say this was one of the more pleasurable Saturday afternoons I've spent."

"You're welcome." Cocking her head, she studied him. "You know, Griffin, for someone who claims not to believe in love, you sure did a good imitation with your explanation to Sammy this afternoon." She'd been both touched and moved by the way he'd handled the young boy, as well as his curiosities and all his questions.

A bit uncomfortable, Griffin shifted his weight, slipping his hands into the pocket of his shorts. "It wasn't that big of a deal, Maggy." He shrugged. "I think it's important that the boy learn what's really important and not judge people by the things they have in their life but rather by *who* they have in their life." His gaze met hers and he thought about his feelings last night, when he realized Maggy might not always be in *his* life. The idea scared him as nothing else ever before had, so he banished the thought for now, not certain what to do about it.

"If you really believe that, Griffin, then why can't you believe that my grandfather is more interested in your grandmother's heart than her money?"

With a long sigh, Griffin glanced off in the distance and shook his head. "Maggy, I know this really bothers you, the fact that I don't believe in romantic love, not really."

"It bothers me more that you think so little of my grandfather."

"It's not him, per se, Maggy, truly." He smiled sheepishly. "I actually like your grandfather, but how would you feel if our roles were reversed, and it was your grandfather who'd heard from an old flame forty years after their last encounter, now, when your grandfather is a very wealthy widower. Wouldn't you feel a bit skeptical?" Griffin shook his head. "Try to understand. I love my grandmother and I don't want to see her hurt."

"I can understand, Griffin," Maggy said carefully, feeling annoyed at him all over again. "Any more than I want to see my grandfather hurt—by anyone, " she added, wishing her voice didn't sound so much like a threat.

"I just want to protect my grandmother, Maggy, can

you understand that?" His gaze searched hers and she nodded. A gentle breeze fluttered in the wind, fluttering her mane of curls.

"Yes, I can understand that. The urge to protect those we love is instinctive and natural. But don't mistake protecting her with preventing her from having a life or love in that life."

Truly disturbed by her words, Griffin looked at her for a moment, examining his conscience. Is that what he'd been doing? Not simply protecting his grandmother, but preventing her from having love or happiness in her life?

The thought both frightened and appalled him.

Is that what he'd been doing to himself? a small voice inside wondered. Had he allowed his own suspicions and distrust of people, women in particular, prevent him from having love in his life?

At the moment, Griffin realized he wasn't entirely certain.

"I know you haven't had many great experiences with love, Griffin, but sometimes love can show up when you least expect it, and with the person you least expect it with." Maggy smiled sadly. "And if we're very lucky, sometimes the person we love loves us in return."

"But for how long?" he couldn't help but ask, bitterness lacing his tone. "Until the money runs out? Or until someone younger and more attractive shows up?" He shook his head, thinking of his father. "Not everyone has honorable intentions, and not everyone who thinks they're in love truly is."

She looked at him for a moment feeling sad and sorry for the experiences he'd had that had robbed him of his ability to trust, or to even believe in love. Then on impulse she leaned forward and kissed him on the cheek. "But that's part of the beauty of love, Griffin, taking a chance and following your heart. That's where trust comes in. You can't love someone without trust, that's the first step to love. I'm sorry that you can't see or understand that." Smiling sadly, she kissed him again, her heart aching for him and for her. "Why don't you come to dinner tomorrow? Three sharp." With that, Maggy let herself in the house with her heart aching, then shut and locked the door quietly behind her.

"Maggy, what time is Grandpa coming home?" Michael asked as he grabbed a cold soda out of the refrigerator and pulled loose his tie, tugging it over his head.

It was Sunday morning, and they'd just returned from church. It was a family tradition. Whoever wasn't working on Sunday congregated at her grandfather's after Sunday mass, then they had dinner promptly at three in the afternoon.

"I'm not sure," Maggy said as she chopped onions for her famous Irish stew. She'd already changed into something comfortable, her usual T-shirt and shorts. "Sometime today. After dinner probably." She glanced over her shoulder at her brother. "I hope you don't mind but I invited Griffin for dinner."

Michael drank deeply from his soda, then sank down in a chair, unbuttoning his collar and rolling up the sleeves of his dress shirt. "I don't mind." He hesitated and she turned to glance at him again.

"What?" she asked at the look on his face. "What's with that look?"

Michael shrugged out of his suit coat. "You haven't invited a man home for Sunday dinner since before you left for college."

"I know," she admitted, reaching for the celery stalks and rinsing them before laying them on a wooden cutting board.

"I thought this was just a business relationship," Michael said with a worried frown.

"It is," Maggy assured him. "But Michael, I don't think Grandpa's relationship with Millicent is business." She turned and flashed him a grin. "I think that one's strictly pleasure, and if it goes where I think it's going, Griffin might become part of the family—indirectly," she added. "And he's not exactly pleased about it, so I thought it would be a good idea for him to meet you guys."

"Sounds fair," Michael said, still worried and not entirely certain Maggy was telling him the whole truth about her own feelings. "So why isn't this guy pleased about Grandpa and Millicent?"

Maggy hesitated. She'd never knowingly lied to her brothers. She hadn't dared since they knew her so well that they'd know in an instant and then there'd be hell to pay, but she seriously considered it just this once, then realized she couldn't do it.

"Griffin thinks Grandpa's only interested in Millicent's money."

Michael threw back his head and laughed. "You've got to be kidding."

"No, I wish I were," she admitted, moving to chop several cloves of garlic before tossing them into the stew pot to simmer along with the onions.

"How can anyone think Grandpa is only interested in money?"

Maggy laughed. "Griffin is a cynic. He hasn't had very many promising experiences with love and doesn't really believe in it. He thinks everyone has an ulterior motive."

"Maggy," Michael said carefully, watching his sister, "you don't have any personal interest in this guy or anything, do you?"

She wished he didn't sound so suspicious and protective. It was always a worrisome sign.

Maggy sighed and set down the chopping knife she'd been using. "I do, Michael," she said, turning to face him and wiping her hands down the apron that covered her. "But I shouldn't.

It was the first time she'd openly admitted that she'd allowed herself to have feelings for Griffin, feelings that she knew she had no place feeling, but it was impossible to tell that to her heart.

Michael frowned. "Okay, I'll bite. Why shouldn't you have feelings for the guy?"

Shaking her head, Maggy crossed the room and pulled out a chair, sitting down next to her brother. "Several reasons. First, like I just said, he's not the kind of man who believes in love or marriage."

"He's a player, then?" Michael asked with a deep frown. In his book, there was nothing worse than a player, someone who merely used women and discarded them. He certainly didn't want someone like that anywhere near his sister.

Maggy almost laughed. "No, nothing like that, Michael. He's just not had any reason to trust many people and he's cynical, suspicious and doesn't believe in love."

"I'll buy that, lots of guys feel that way." He grinned suddenly. "Until they meet the right woman."

"No, I don't think that's the case with Griffin. I don't think he believes there is such a thing as the 'right' woman. I think he thinks they're all not to be trusted."

"Even you?" Michael asked carefully, wondering if he and his brothers would have to have a talk with this guy. How could anyone not trust Maggy? Anyone who knew her loved and trusted her. And then not to trust his grandfather, well, that was unthinkable. His grandfather was the salt of the earth and had more honor and integrity than any ten other men put together.

"Especially me," she said quietly. "More important, Michael, like Dennis, Griffin's the kind of man who grew up surrounded by wealth and privilege, the kind who's so comfortable moving and living in that upscale world he lives in, where limos and personal shoppers are just an everyday part of his life, that he doesn't realize not everyone fits into that lifestyle." Maggy shook her head. "I tried that once, remember? I tried being a wife to that kind of man and it just didn't work out. Dennis made it clear that I would never fit or be accepted in his world. That's not me, Michael. I don't want a driver, I want to do my own shopping, and I want to be me. Just me. With no pretense about who or what I am." Resting her chin on her hand, she glanced up at him glumly. "So, yes, I have feelings for him. And no, he doesn't have any for me, or won't allow himself to have any for me, and even if he did, in some ways, he's just like Dennis, so why on earth would I want to make the same mistake twice?" she asked with a dismal shake of her head.

"Dennis was an idiot," Michael said, draining his soda and getting to his feet. "Not all men with money are idiots, sis." He tossed his empty can to the recycling bin tucked into one corner of the kitchen. "Some are actually decent." He grabbed his suit coat off the back of the chair. "I'm going to go change before everyone else gets here."

"Fine." Maggy got up. "I'll finish getting the stew going."

"Are you making dumplings?"

Maggy grinned. "What's Irish stew without homemade dumplings?"

"Boring," Michael said, giving her a kiss on the cheek. "Be right back." Heading out of the kitchen, Michael decided perhaps it was a good thing Maggy had invited Griffin. It would give him and his brothers a chance to assess him and the situation, and make whatever adjustments they thought necessary.

Michael grinned. It had been a long time since he and his brothers had to correct some wayward male's thinking, but when it came to their sister, or their grandfather, one thing was certain—the Gallagher men didn't stand on ceremony.

Now, all he had to do was make sure Maggy didn't find out or they'd all be in serious trouble.

"Griffin," Michael said, glancing at the man across the cluttered dining-room table. They'd just finished a rather lively dinner, discussing everything from politics to the affairs in Northern Ireland. To Michael's surprise he found he liked Griffin. In spite of Maggy's claims about who he was and how he'd grown up, he seemed like just a regular guy to him.

"After Sunday dinner my brothers and I usually play a pickup game of basketball out back." Michael grinned benevolently, leaning back in his chair. "We usually do three-on-two, especially when Maggy won't play with us, but since you're here, we could make a real game of it. Three against three. Think you'd be interested? We'll even spot you ten points. It'll be me, Collin and Finn against you and the twins, Tyler and Trace."

Maggy wanted to roll her eyes as she rose to pour the coffee. Macho stuff again. Clearly her brothers didn't realize that not every man in the universe was a sports nut. Or athletically inclined.

She had a feeling that, during his college days, Griffin had been dedicated to his studies and not to scoring points on some field or court.

"Michael, Griffin's a lawyer, I seriously doubt if he plays basketball," she said, glaring at her brother and instantly leaping to defend Griffin so he wouldn't be embarrassed.

"Is that a fact, Maggy?" Griffin asked with a lift of his eyebrow, leaning back in his chair like Michael as he looked from one of her brothers to the others.

Six in all. Hard to believe there were so many members of this family with so many different personalities.

While all her brothers looked unbelievably alike with their tall, muscular frames, inky-black hair and large green eyes, they each had some identifiable feature that allowed him to memorize quickly who was who, especially the twins, Tyler and Trace.

Tyler, who sat directly across the table from Griffin, was a Chicago fireman and wore a small gold cross earring in his ear. Trace, who was seated next to Griffin, was also a fireman and wore a gold cross medallion around his neck and no earring at all. They were the youngest of the brood and treated as such.

Collin was seated next to Tyler. He was also a fireman, and had a few scars on his left hand and a few along the side of his neck to prove it.

Finn, who was seated at the head of the dining-room table at the chair that was traditionally their grandfather's seat, was just a hair taller than Michael, although he was a year younger. But he was also a cop, like Michael, and the two of them worked undercover out of the same precinct. Finn was the only one of the boys to have a dimple in his chin, giving him a fairly recognizable look.

Patrick Jr., named after his grandfather, was also a cop and he was easy to tell apart from the others simply because he was the shortest, if you considered six foot two short. But compared to his brothers, he looked like a munchkin.

Griffin thought he'd be uncomfortable having dinner with Maggy and her brothers, but he'd found it to be a wonderfully pleasant experience. He'd never actually had a big family dinner like this before, since growing up it had only been him and his grandparents, and on Sundays, they generally went out to dinner.

To his surprise, he found himself actually joining in and enjoying the camaraderie that came from the different men and the different relationships they had with each other, as well as with Maggy.

All in all, Griffin decided, this had been a wonderful way to spend a Sunday afternoon, much better than having dinner alone with a book, which was something he usually did on Sundays.

"Michael," Maggy said again, a clear warning in her voice. "I'm sure there's something other than basketball Griffin would like to do this afternoon."

Unconsciously, Griffin put his hand on Maggy's arm, absently stroking to soothe her ruffled feathers, unaware that six sets of eyes saw his action and exchanged silent, inquisitive looks that said more than words.

It tickled him that she would so readily jump to his defense, and that she so readily assumed he was a man who didn't enjoy or participate in sports.

"Actually, Maggy, I'd love to play." Griffin stroked her arm, unaware of the shivers he sent racing over her. She almost dropped the coffeepot again. "But you've got me at a disadvantage," he said to Michael, earning a grin. "It's been a long time since I've played a game of hoops."

"You know how to play basketball?" Maggy asked in surprise, turning to him and watching a slow, sly smile spread across his features. The man drank beer and knew how to play basketball. He was ruining every single image she had of him being a seriously stuffed shirt, not to mention a snob.

"A little," Griffin said. He grinned up at Maggy who was busily pouring coffee for Collin. "Actually, Maggy, I…uh…went to college on a full basketball scholarship," he finally admitted.

Michael sat forward. "A full ride?" He shook his head, wondering if he should retract his ten-point spotting offer.

Shock had Maggy almost bobbling the coffeepot. "Easy, Maggy," her brother Collin said with a grin, reaching out a hand to steady the pot for her before he had it dumped in his lap.

"Where'd you go to school?" Trace, the youngest of the twins asked Griffin before Maggy had a chance to open her mouth, leaning forward in his chair.

Tongue in cheek, Griffin tried to appear nonchalant. "University of Arizona."

"You were a Wildcat?" Tyler, Maggy's other twin brother asked, his eyes widening in delight.

"Absolutely," Griffin confirmed with a nod of his head, watching Maggy's brothers exchange looks.

"He bushwhacked us," Michael groaned to Finn, who was grinning like a loon.

"Totally," Finn agreed, taking a sip of his coffee.

"Hey," Griffin protested good-naturedly with a grin of his own, lifting his hands up in the air. "You're the one who spotted me the points." Relaxed, he leaned back in his chair, hooking his arm over the back. "You should have asked if I could play before you spotted me." He turned to the twins. "Right, guys?"

"Absolutely," Tyler and Trace said in unison, their dark heads bobbing up and down. They could already smell victory and Griffin's stock went up several points in their eyes.

"Wait a minute." Maggy set the coffeepot down on the dining-room table hard enough to get everyone's attention. "I don't understand. Will someone please explain to me what's going on?" She turned to Michael and pointed. "You, how did Griffin bushwhack you? You said you'd give him ten points, it's not like he asked for them." She turned to Finn. "And why are you grinning like that?" She crossed her arms over her chest. "Someone explain to me what's going on."

"Sweetheart," Finn said, reaching for her hand and affectionately tugging her down on his lap. "It seems that your friend Griffin here is a Michael Jordan protégé, so to speak."

She frowned, glancing at Griffin, then back to her brother. "Excuse me?"

Finn laughed, adjusting her more comfortably on his lap. "The University of Arizona has historically had one of the best basketball programs in the country. This year, even before the season began they were ranked number one in the country."

"And this means…what?" she asked, still not understanding.

"This means," Collin filled in, "that they have one of the best basketball programs in the country because they recruit the best players in the country."

Maggy glanced at Griffin, trying to picture this man driving down the basketball court, arms and elbows flying, sweat dripping. Nope, she just couldn't picture it.

"Griffin was such a good player, sis," Finn went on, "that Arizona gave him a full scholarship to play basketball for them."

"As opposed to any other college in the country," Michael added with what sounded like a groan.

"Which simply means, Griffin was one of the best basketball players in the country," Finn finished with a grin.

"You really do know how to play basketball, then?" she asked in surprise, turning to Griffin and making Michael and Patrick Jr. as well as the twins groan.

"Yeah, I do know how to play a little basketball," he admitted.

She turned to Michael. "And you think he bushwhacked you because he didn't tell you that *before* you spotted him ten points?"

"Yep," Michael said with a weary sigh. "That's the general idea."

"Michael, I'm sorry, but you're an idiot," she said, making everyone at the table laugh. "Didn't it occur to you to ask the man if he could play basketball *before* you gave him the ten points?"

With a laugh and a shake of his head, Michael pushed himself up and away from the table, bending to kiss her cheek. "That's why you're the advice columnist, sis, and I'm just a cop." He glanced at Griffin. "Shall we go shoot a few?" he asked, anxious to see Griffin play. Michael companionably draped an arm around Griffin's shoulder. "You know, we could really use you on our league, Griffin. It's a group of cops versus the fireman. We have a regular team schedule." Michael grinned. "We lost the league championship by two points last year, but with a little help, I'm sure we could bring that trophy home." Michael wiggled his eyebrows. "Know what I mean?"

"Hey, Michael, that's not fair," Trace complained. "You're recruiting out of the ranks."

"Kid, all's fair in love and basketball." With a laugh,

Finn draped his own arm around his younger brother. "And if you don't believe me, ask Grandpa," he said with a laugh.

"Hey, wait a minute," Maggy said, hands on hips as they filed out of the dining room, ignoring her. "Who's going to help me with these dishes?"

After the table was cleared, the food put away and the dishes done, Maggy sat down at the kitchen table and began reading and sorting some more of Aunt Millie's letters, wanting to get a head start on the week.

Through the open kitchen window, she could hear the basketball game in progress. The sound of shouts and good-natured male curses drifted into the kitchen, making her smile.

If anyone had ever told her Griffin would be playing basketball with her brothers on a sunny Sunday afternoon she would have laughed in their face.

But that's exactly what was going on, she thought, getting up from the table to peek out the window. She had hoped that meeting her brothers would calm Griffin's worries about her grandfather. Surely any man who'd raised seven reasonably responsible adults couldn't have a malicious or vicious bone in his body. More than anything, she wanted Griffin to see her grandfather for who and what he really was, and not be overshadowed by Griffin's own miserable past and inbred distrust.

Not certain if her plan had worked or not, Maggy turned to head back to the kitchen table, to get back to her own work, when she heard the collision of hard male bodies, a loud crash, and then an even louder muttered curse before the sound of running feet took over once again.

She wasn't going to look, she told herself as she plopped down in her chair. Still, she cast a worried glance behind her at the window before returning her attention to the pile of letters she'd laid out.

During the first few weeks she'd been shadowing Millicent she'd learned a great deal about the process that kept "Aunt Millie" on track. All mail was received, opened and sorted in the morning—some mornings they didn't finish, even though Millicent explained that she usually hired temporary assistants to do the sorting when she got behind, but while Maggy was shadowing her, she wanted Maggy to see the entire process so she'd have a clear understanding of it. In the event Maggy decided to take over the column permanently, Millicent wanted her to be able to develop a work schedule that was comfortable for her.

Afternoons were spent answering mail, typing up the responses, contacting professionals for expert advice or opinions. All letters were answered whether they appeared in the newspaper or not.

The ones chosen to be published were generally letters that would help more than just the author of the letter, thus, most of the letters published dealt with universal issues that could relate to any number of people.

In spite of the enormous workload, Maggy had to admit that being Aunt Millie was both invigorating and exciting, if only she didn't have to go to all those social engagements and pretend to be someone or something she wasn't, then she'd have truly enjoyed being Aunt Millie.

All of the columns were done five weeks in advance, giving Millicent enough lead time to account for illness or vacation. Even when Millicent was ill or on vacation, the column appeared.

Although Maggy had learned the basic procedures, all of the business dealings for Aunt Millie, including contracts and legal matters, were handled exclusively by Griffin and his law firm.

Millicent had told her early on that the only thing she would insist upon with whoever took over her column was that Griffin's firm still handle all contracts and legal transactions, simply because Millicent herself would retain ownership and all rights, including copyright to the "Aunt Millie" column and persona.

At the time, it hadn't bothered Maggy, but now, she realized, it was something she had to seriously think about.

Tapping a pen absently against her lip as she reread the same letter for the third time, Maggy realized that even though she hadn't made a decision yet about the column, she'd have to take into consideration that if she did decide to do this on a permanent basis, Griffin would be a part of her life permanently.

And how on earth could she work with him on a daily basis, knowing how she felt about him, but also knowing he'd never allow himself to feel the same way in return?

She simply didn't know.

In the past few weeks, the more she'd gotten to know him, the more she'd known her feelings for him were growing and she was powerless to stop them. He'd touched and softened her heart with his kindness, his generosity and his goodness.

With a sigh, Maggy shook her head. But she also knew her own growing feelings could not amount to anything simply because nothing could erase the fact that they came from two different worlds.

And it just wouldn't work between them, at least not on a personal basis. She'd known that from the moment she'd lain eyes on him. Unfortunately, someone forgot to tell her wary heart.

In spite of the fact that Griffin had seemed too much like Dennis, at least on the outside, on the inside she knew that Griffin wasn't like Dennis at all.

And she hadn't a clue what to do about it, or her aching heart. Even if they did somehow manage to bridge the gap between his world and her own, she knew that Griffin didn't trust her—or any woman—enough to allow himself to let his heart go and just love.

And knowing that Griffin didn't trust her and wouldn't allow himself to love her almost broke her heart.

Dear Aunt Millie:

I'm thirty-two and have been dating Wilbur for ten years. Wilbur is thirty-nine and lives at home with his widowed mother. We've talked about getting married, but Wilbur says he's still not sure if I'm the one. Quite frankly, I'm tired of waiting. I've been offered a fabulous promotion at work, but it would require a transfer to sunny California, almost three thousand miles away. I told Wilbur, but he doesn't want me to take the job, nor does he know when he'll be ready to make a decision about marriage. After all this time, I'm not sure what to do. Please help.

Confused in Connecticut

Dear Confused:

If a man doesn't know if you're the right one after ten years, he'll never know. Take the promotion and leave Wilbur with his mother. You deserve to be happy and to have a man who really wants to be with you, not one who needs to be coaxed into it. Go, and don't look back, dear. The best and next part of your life is waiting for you in sunny California and I'll bet

a new romance will be along shortly as well. Enjoy your new job and your new life, dear. You deserve it!
    Aunt Millie

Chapter Nine

On Monday afternoon, Griffin was surprised to find himself back at the Plantation restaurant, at his grandmother's request. When he arrived though, he was taken aback to find Patrick with her.

"Ah, laddie, I'm so glad you could join us." With a hearty smile, Patrick pulled out a chair for Griffin, nerves making his knees knock as he glanced over at Millicent with an indulgent smile.

"Thank you for inviting me," Griffin said warily. "Grandmother," he said, leaning over to kiss her cheek before taking his own seat across from her. "Did you enjoy your weekend away?" he forced himself to ask.

"Yes, we had a fine old time," she said. Patrick sat, then reached for Millicent's hand, holding on tight. "Millicent and I...well..." Never at a loss for words, Patrick finally found himself speechless for the first time in his life as emotions backed up from his heart, filling his throat.

"Griffin darling," Millicent began with a sweet, indulgent smile as she patted Patrick's hand in comfort. "Patrick has asked me to marry him and I've accepted."

"Married!" Griffin exclaimed, stunned, nearly knocking over his water glass. "What do you mean he's asked you to marry him and you've accepted. That's…ludicrous, Grandmother, simply ludicrous."

Millicent stiffened and her eyes went cold. "Excuse me, Griffin, but exactly what's ludicrous about it? I love Patrick and he loves me." Millicent shrugged, trying to hide her hurt and anger over her grandson's response. "Why shouldn't we marry?"

How could he have not seen this coming? ~~Patrick~~ Griffin wondered. How had he let the old man bushwhack him and his grandmother? Because he'd been so involved with Maggy, that he hadn't been paying attention to the things he should have.

Like his grandmother's welfare.

Had Maggy deliberately kept him occupied so that he wouldn't realize what was going on? he wondered. Had she deliberately deceived him, knowing this was what her grandfather had planned all along?

"Uh, Griffin my lad, I brought along something that I thought might show that my intentions are honorable."

Griffin frowned, confused, angry and feeling horribly, terribly betrayed. "What are you talking about, Patrick?"

Patrick pulled a sheaf of folded papers from his breast pocket. "My lawyer said to give these to you." He slid the papers across the table.

"Patrick," Millicent scolded. "I told you that wasn't necessary."

He patted her hand. "Aye, love, I know, but you see,

sometimes it's important to extend trust before you ask for it," Patrick said, deliberately glancing at Griffin.

"This…this is a prenuptial agreement," Griffin said dully, reading quickly and trying to absorb everything.

"Aye, that it is, laddie."

Stunned, Griffin glanced up at Patrick. "It says that you're forever relinquishing any rights to any of my grandmother's wealth and assets, including any intellectual property as well as any real property now and forever."

"Aye, laddie, I know what it says," Patrick said with a grin, lifting his wine for a sip. "I'm the one who told the lawyer what to put into it."

"It also says that you intend to support and care for my grandmother solely on your income and assets from the day of your marriage forward."

"Aye, that's true, as well, laddie."

"You mean you really don't have any interest in her money?" Griffin asked, feeling both relieved and more than a bit embarrassed.

"Nay, laddie, not a whit." Patrick grinned, then leaned across the table to speak quietly to Griffin. "I don't like discussing these things in front of my future wife, laddie, but I thought you should know I've got a fair amount of money of me own put away." He winked and pushed another sheaf of papers at Griffin as he nodded toward Millicent. "Don't want her to know, though, since I want to be certain she's marrying me for me and my good looks and not for my wealth." Patrick winked again. "You know how these things go, laddie boy."

Griffin opened the second sheaf of papers and read a one-week-old printout from one of the most prestigious stockbrokers in the city. "Patrick, you're…rich?" he said weakly.

"Aye, if I have to confess, I will. I am, laddie. Got more

money than I know what to do with, which is why I just put it into all those fancy trusts and brokerage accounts, so I don't have to worry about it."

He lifted his gaze to his grandmother, saw the hurt and disappointment in her eyes, then shifted his gaze to Patrick, overwhelmed by emotion. Fear drained immediately as did his anger, leaving him feeling empty and hollow.

What had Patrick said about extending trust before expecting it?

That was a lesson he'd do well to remember.

He'd been so wrong, Griffin realized. About so many things. Never in his life had he ever felt like such a fool. Maggy had told him repeatedly that her grandfather wasn't interested in his grandmother's money, but he hadn't believed her. Hadn't trusted Maggy or Patrick enough to believe that what Patrick felt for his grandmother was real love. But now, looking at them, even a blind man could see the love, bright and clear, shimmering between them.

Love.

How often had he seen it in his life? he wondered. How often had he even paid attention?

What had Maggy said about love sneaking up on you when you least expected it, and with someone you least expected?

He should have trusted her, he realized, feeling guilty and more than a bit ashamed. Unlike Marissa and every other woman he'd encountered, Maggy had been honest with him from day one about everything, he realized. She hadn't lied or deceived him, nor anyone.

"Patrick, please allow me to apologize." Still a bit stunned, Griffin shook his head. "It certainly doesn't excuse my behavior—"

"No, it doesn't," Millicent said quietly.

Duly chastised and embarrassed, Griffin nodded. "But please know, Patrick, it wasn't personal. I would have been suspicious of anyone who I thought was trying to romance my grandmother."

"Aye, laddie, no apologies are necessary. 'Tis a good thing my little Millie here has had someone looking out after her since your grandfather's passing. I don't fault you at all, son, and would have expected no less from you." Patrick winked. "When we love someone, laddie, we do what we can to see that no one or nothing every hurts them." Patrick shrugged. "It's only natural, but sometimes it makes us behave like…like a donkey's rear. But aye, it's good to always remember the reason, nothing we ever do for love is foolish or to be ashamed of, laddie. You were protecting your grandmother because you love her, son, nothing more, nothing less, and I wouldn't have expected any less."

"Does Maggy know?" Griffin asked, letting his gaze shift from Patrick to his grandmother.

"Yes, Griffin, we told her late last night when we returned from Lake Geneva." Millicent smiled indulgently at Patrick, giving his hand a loving squeeze. "And she's delighted," Millicent added meaningfully. "She knows how rare it is to find love, let alone have it returned. You'd do well to remember that, Griffin," Millicent said softly, glancing at Patrick. "Love is so rare, and makes life so very, very sweet, darling, that once you find it, it's best to hold on to it with both hands." She shifted her gaze to her grandson. "Do you understand what I mean, dear?" his grandmother asked pointedly.

His logical mind didn't believe in love—it couldn't believe in something he'd never experienced or witnessed—something that was so clearly not permanent, but fickle and futile.

Looking at his grandmother and Patrick he wasn't so

certain he wasn't witnessing it now. Between them he saw the same joy and contentedness he'd once only seen between his grandfather and grandmother.

But now, his grandmother had found that kind of love again, the kind that apparently filled her heart with joy and her eyes with happiness.

Had he ever felt that way? he wondered. Had he ever allowed himself to feel that way?

Not until he'd met Maggy.

But he couldn't and wouldn't express such feelings. He couldn't, not knowing how Maggy felt about him, not knowing that she'd vowed never again to love someone who wasn't from "her" world.

He wasn't from her world and knew he never could be. That didn't change who he was but only who he wanted to be—for her.

He wasn't certain he could define what he felt for Maggy as love, but he knew it was something he'd never felt before. There was an inherent trust involved, something he'd never allowed another woman. A trust that told him that she'd never deceive him, hadn't she said that to him? Hadn't she told him she didn't make a habit of lying to anyone?

In all this time, he'd actually come to believe her, to trust what she'd told him, and that alone was cause for worry, because in trusting her, he feared that he had fallen in love with Maggy.

"Are you relieved that your month as Aunt Millie is finally over?" Griffin asked as he opened the double doors to the Grand Ballroom where the evening gala was being held. Music filled the air, drifting toward them as Maggy came to a halt, scanning the room, knowing the proper social procedure by heart now.

"I don't know if *relieved* is the right word," she said softly, glancing up at him, trying to memorize every single line and feature of his face, knowing after tonight she might never see him again and at the moment, she simply couldn't bear the thought. "I'm glad this is the last black-tie social function I have to attend, though."

"You really hate these things, don't you?" he asked, taking her hand to lead her across the room toward their assigned table.

"Yes, Griffin, I'm afraid I do. I told you, I'm not interested in pretending to be something I'm not. I tried that once, remember? It didn't work, and I'm not someone who makes the same mistakes twice." With a nod of her head, she acknowledged a society reporter who'd interviewed her just last week.

She was right about that, he thought. Maggy was far too pragmatic and practical to make the same mistakes twice, and she'd already married a man she thought was just like him. She hadn't had to say it; he knew it.

And it brought an unbearable ache to his heart, knowing that he, too, had probably hurt Maggy by his lack of trust in her and her grandfather as well as by his lack of belief in both of them.

"I had lunch with your grandfather and my grandmother this afternoon," he said carefully, pulling out her chair for her. "They told me about their engagement."

Maggy stiffened, waiting for the explosion she was certain was coming. "And?" she asked with a lift of her eyebrow, raising the hem of her gown a bit to take her seat.

"I'm delighted for them."

"Delighted," Maggy said, all but goggling at him. "You're delighted that my grandfather, a man you don't trust as far as you can see, is going to marry your grandmother?" Wonders would never cease, she decided, if Griffin had finally decided her grandfather was on the level.

Griffin shrugged, then took his own seat. "Well, Maggy, it's kind of hard not to believe or trust when you see how happy and how in love they are."

"In love," she repeated with a shake of her head. "How on earth would a man who doesn't believe in love recognize it?"

He laughed. "That's a fair question," he said, standing and extending his hand to her. "But maybe that's because I haven't actually seen it before, at least not since my grandfather's death, but I can see it now when I look at the two of them." He hesitated. "May I have this dance?"

She was still sitting there, staring at him openmouthed. "Dance?" Maggy shook her head. "You want to dance now?"

"Well, since this is your last social engagement as Aunt Millie, I think the least we can do is try to enjoy ourselves, don't you?" With a smile, Griffin led Maggy onto the dance floor, anxious to hold her in his arms one last time.

The street Maggy lived on was dark and quiet when Ernie pulled the car to a halt in front of her house. The temperature had dropped in the past few weeks so there was a hint of fall in the air. The leaves had begun changing colors and were now drifting slowly toward the ground.

"Thank you very much, Griffin, for everything." Maggy hesitated. She had no idea if she'd see Griffin again after tonight. His role shadowing her was over as well as was her own role shadowing Aunt Millie.

"Griffin," she began, causing him to turn and look at her. "I want you to know how very much I appreciate all you've done for me during this time I've been shadowing your grandmother."

He lifted her hand and brought it to his lips for a kiss, sending a heated shiver racing up and down her arm. "It was my pleasure, Maggy." He kissed her hand again. "My pleasure, indeed."

Maggy sighed, not sure how to proceed. "You know, this went much faster than I anticipated."

"It did, didn't it?" he murmured, still holding her hand and drawing her close. "I'm going to miss this," he said softly, pressing a kiss to her cheek, then letting his lips linger to travel down her face to tease the corner of her lips.

With her pulse scrambling, Maggy tried to concentrate on what she wanted to say to him, but his lips were distracting her.

"And you, Maggy, I'm going to miss you."

His words caused her to still. This time when her pulse sped up it wasn't from desire but purely from fear.

He was saying goodbye, she realized. Saying he wasn't planning on seeing her again after tonight. The ache in her fragile, scarred heart was like a sharp stiletto piercing it, allowing the pain to seep through her pores into every inch of her being.

How on earth could she have so foolishly fallen in love with a man she knew she had no business loving?

She wanted to tell him he wouldn't have to miss her, that they could continue seeing each other, but she knew better. She knew there was no point since he wasn't interested in loving her and it broke her shattered heart just a little bit more.

She may have fallen foolishly in love with him, but that didn't mean Griffin had done anything quite so foolish as fall in love with someone like her.

As it was, he'd already told her he didn't believe in love. More important, for the past month whenever they were together, she'd been playing at being someone else, someone who fit and moved easily in his world, was accepted in his world.

But that wasn't her. She wasn't the woman who drove around in limos or had leisurely hundred-dollar lunches in fashionably private clubs.

So why on earth would she have expected him to fall in love with her? Someone who clearly didn't fit or move in his world. He was who he'd always been, and now she would go back to who she really was, and that wasn't someone Griffin could apparently take seriously or love.

Hadn't he told her he didn't really believe in something as fragile and fleeting as love anyway?

He'd told her, but she hadn't really believed him.

Until now.

Trying to hold back her tears, Maggy forced a smile. "Well, I'll miss you, too, Griffin," she said as casually as she could. "But won't you be at the dinner Saturday night? When I give your grandmother my final answer?"

He frowned. He'd been concentrating on Maggy's scent, on the beautiful line of her bare, slender shoulders. "Actually, Maggy, I think it might be a good idea for you to meet with my grandmother yourself."

She heard his words, and once again felt as if a stiletto had gone through her heart. He didn't even want to be there when she gave his grandmother her final answer. He was done with his duties, and now couldn't wait to dismiss her.

Forcing herself to hold her tears in check, she leaned over and kissed him, allowing herself a few moments to savor this one last kiss. "If you don't mind, Griffin, I've got a headache." She touched her forehead, realizing it was true. "I think I'm going to go in."

"All right." Disappointed, he looked at her. "You looked absolutely beautiful tonight, Maggy. Just breathtaking."

"Thanks." She managed a smile, certain her face was going to crack as easily as her heart just had. She glanced down at herself. "I have to admit it will be nice not to have to wear all these fancy-dancy duds anymore." Breathing a sigh of relief, she turned to him. "I can go back to my jeans and T-shirts."

"You look beautiful no matter what you wear," he said, meaning it.

Maggy laughed. "Thank you, Griffin, but somehow I have a feeling that my definition of beautiful and yours might be a tad different." She knew he was used to truly astounding society women who had nothing to do all day but have their personal shoppers hunt for just the perfect gown while they whiled away their time having leisurely lunches at exclusive salons and private clubs.

That wasn't her, and never could be, she knew because she'd tried it once and failed miserably.

She smiled, then touched her forehead again. She wanted to get this over with. It was just far too painful knowing she wouldn't see him again, at least not on a personal or social basis.

"Come on, Maggy, let's get you inside." Griffin threw open the door and came around to help her out. When she took his hand, Maggy made a mental note of it, savoring every single sensation, wanting only to keep the memories safe inside her, knowing after tonight she'd have little more than memories.

"Shall I walk you up?" he asked, glancing at the darkened windows in her apartment.

"No, thanks, Griffin. It's late, and I'm sure Grandpa is asleep." She flashed him a small smile, knowing she couldn't hold back her tears much longer. "I can manage."

"Good night, then, Maggy." He slid his arms around her and pulled her close, brushing his lips tenderly across hers.

He heard her small moan, and drew her closer, wanting to feel the warmth of her seep into him, into every crevice and cranny that had always been so cold and empty without her. He watched her walk away and knew something wonderful had just walked out of his life, leaving him both sad and sorry.

Millicent nervously sipped her wine as she waited for Maggy and Patrick. She'd chosen a small Italian restaurant in Patrick's neighborhood to have this dinner in. She wanted Maggy to be completely comfortable and at ease, as well as Patrick, when Maggy gave her the final decision. Her face brightened when she saw Patrick lead Maggy into the restaurant.

"Millie girl, you look beautiful," Patrick said, leaning down to peck her on the cheek. "As usual."

She reached for his hand and gave it a squeeze. "Thank you, Patrick dear."

"Maggy, I don't know if you'd like to have dinner first, or get our discussion over with first?" Millicent asked quietly, aware of how tense she and Maggy both were.

Maggy hesitated for just a moment. Thoughts of Griffin had occupied her for most of the past few days, but she had to concentrate on tonight, on what she was going to say to Millicent, but just being here with Millicent made her miss Griffin all the more.

"Actually, Millicent, I'm so nervous I don't think I could eat right now. Do you think we can eat later?"

"Of course, dear." Millicent folded her hands on the table. She glanced at Maggy hopefully.

"Millicent," Maggy began slowly, wondering just how Griffin was going to take *her* news. So much of her life had changed, every part of her life had changed because of Millicent and Griffin, she just wished she hadn't fallen in love with him. "You know I agreed to shadow you for thirty days to simply try things out as Aunt Millie?"

"Yes, dear, I know," Millicent said hopefully, holding on tight to Patrick's hand.

"I never expected to enjoy it," Maggy admitted with a smile. "I never expected to find it so fulfilling or rewarding. But I did." She laughed suddenly. "I'm not going to tell you I enjoy the socializing because I don't, simply because I'm not really comfortable in that world," Maggy admitted without shame. "It makes me feel like I'm pretending to be someone I'm not, and I don't think that's a good thing for Aunt Millie."

Millicent nodded. "You know, Maggy, I think you're quite right. How can others trust Aunt Millie to be honest if she's not being honest with herself?"

"Exactly," Maggy said, fingering the stem of her wineglass, aware that Millicent was watching her carefully. "So, I've made a decision, but I don't know if it's the one you were hoping for."

"I'll accept whatever your decision is, dear," Millicent said kindly, reaching across the table to touch Maggy's hand. "As I've told you, you've done a magnificent job. I couldn't have chosen a better, more qualified successor even if it was only for thirty days."

Maggy took a deep breath. "Millicent, I'm going to accept your offer to become Aunt Millie, but on the condition that I not be required to attend those society gigs." Maggy hesitated. She'd thought about this so long and hard, thought about how much she enjoyed being able to make a difference in someone's life. "I'm just not comfortable trying to be something I'm not, moving in a world where I'm not comfortable, nor where I think I fit in. I think that Aunt Millie—the new Aunt Millie—should be a reflection of today's woman—every woman. And how many women really have the time, the money or the energy to go out socializing on that scale several times a week? Not many," Maggy said with a confirmed nod of her head.

"Aunt Millie has to be someone seen as having the same problems as everyone else. How else will other people be able to understand and relate to her, and more important, ask her for help or advice?" Maggy leaned forward. "I think part of Aunt Millie's success has been the fact that, as you said, when you started you were naive, inexperienced and very much like I am right now, struggling to make your own way. I think that's what a lot of women do, but I don't think the average woman is going to want advice from Aunt Millie if they think she's some highbrow, highfalutin society maven who flits from one expensive social gala to another. Women won't be able to relate to her, nor will they trust her, since they won't be able to see her as having any real problems, and I think if we lose that, we lose the essence of who Aunt Millie really is as well as the very heart of the column."

Stunned, Millicent merely stared at Maggy for a long, silent moment until Maggy grew uncomfortable, feeling she'd spoken out of turn. "I'm sorry if I insulted you," Maggy said quietly, realizing her mouth may have finally have done her in. "But you know I always have to be honest."

"Indeed," Millicent said with a broad smile. "Am I insulted?" Millicent laughed. "No, dear, I'm stunned, pleased and impressed by your assessment. Griffin informs me that the latest market shares show our circulation has gone down in the past five years. Slowly, of course, but down nonetheless. I think you may have figured out the reason," Millicent said to Maggy.

"I told you the girl was bright, aye, didn't I, love?" Patrick said proudly, giving Millicent's hand a squeeze.

"You did indeed, dear." Millicent beamed at him.

"So, I've given you my decision," Maggy said, holding her breath. "But you need to give me yours. If you're not comfortable with me taking over the column this way, without any social requirements, then I'll understand completely."

Millicent shook her head. "No, dear. I'm perfectly happy and accept your offer. And I'm thrilled, Maggy, absolutely thrilled. I couldn't be happier. Welcome aboard, dear." Millicent lifted her wineglass to toast Maggy. "To the new Aunt Millie. Long may she reign."

Maggy lifted her own glass, but thoughts of Griffin filled her mind and her aching heart.

Maggy couldn't sleep.

Finally, Sunday morning just after dawn, she got up, threw on some old clothes and grabbed her gardening pail and tools, determined to take her mind off of her aching heart by doing a little physical work in her garden.

The cool fall weather was moving in quickly now, and she needed to get her garden ready for the long, cold winter ahead.

Kneeling in the garden, in a patch of warm, late-September sunlight, Maggy didn't bother to glance up when she heard the backyard gate squeak open, then squeak shut again. Someone was always cutting through their yard, so it certainly wasn't cause for alarm.

But her ears perked up when she heard footsteps heading toward her.

Certain she was letting her imagination get the best of her, Maggy continued repotting her basil plant, letting the cool, rich dirt slide between her fingers, humming softly until the toes of a pair of elegant black imported Italian loafers came into her line of vision.

Her head came up and she pushed her gardening hat back farther on her head so she could see him. Her mouth fell open when she saw Griffin standing in front of her dressed in casual khaki pants, navy blue polo shirt and a pair of expensive sunglasses.

"Griffin." Still tilting her head back to look at him, she had to swallow to find her voice since her heart was pounding like an out-of-control jackhammer. "What are y-you doing here?" she stammered, clutching her trowel tightly in her hand.

"I understand you're the next Aunt Millie," he said, glancing down at her. She looked beautiful. Absolutely, totally beautiful.

Maggy wanted to sigh. So that's why he was here. No doubt to accuse her of lying to him about her intentions.

"Yes, Griffin, I am." Still tilting her head to look at him, she started to stand but he extended a hand to her to help her up. Cautiously, she took it, knowing his mere touch would start her heart and pulse thrumming.

It did.

"I…um…" She had to swallow again before meeting his gaze. She swiped her hands down her shorts, hoping to stop the tingling his touch had caused. "I accepted your grandmother's very generous offer, but with the stipulation that I not have to attend all of those society social functions." She blew out a breath when he just kept looking at her. "I'm sorry if you think I was dishonest with you, Griffin. I wasn't. Truly. I really had no intention of taking over the column when all of this started." She shrugged. "But then as time went on, I realized how much I enjoyed it, and how much I enjoyed helping people. I really think I can make a difference, Griffin, and that's something that's very important to me."

He smiled at her and her pulse leaped. "You're good at it, Maggy. Very good. I think you should have accepted."

Stunned, she merely stared at him as he pulled off his sunglasses and looped them through the buttonhole of his shirt. "But I'm not here about the column."

"You're not?" With her eyes drinking him in, her hands began to itch to touch him, to hold him, to feel his body pressed against hers, but she knew her desire was futile.

"No." He smiled, stepping over her potted plant to step closer to her. "I'm here because I have a problem for Aunt Millie."

"A problem," she said in confusion as he reached in his pants pocket and extracted a letter.

"Yes. I think this letter will explain everything." He handed her the letter. "Read it. Please?" His heart was in his mouth, his eyes, and he wished he had his sunglasses on so she couldn't see the havoc his nerves were playing.

Maggy opened the letter and began reading aloud, her eyes widening and her heart pounding as tears all but blurred the words on the page.

Dear Aunt Millie:

I'm afraid I've been a fool. I met a wonderful, beautiful woman, a woman of character and integrity, and my own foolish pride, fears and distrust caused me to lose her and I don't know what to do. I only know that I love her, and believe we can make and have a wonderful life together, if only she'll give me another chance. She's not interested in living in my world, and doesn't believe I can live in her world, but I don't see why we can't create our own world, just for the two of us. How can I get my lady back and convince her that I love her and want to spend my life with her—and only her.

Slow in Chicago

"Griffin." Tears welled then spilled down Maggy's face. "Oh, Griffin."

He closed the distance between them in a flash, hauling her off her feet and into his arms, holding her tightly against him as he brought his lips to hers. "Maggy, Maggy, I was so frightened I'd lost you. That it was too late." He rained kisses over her face, her eyes, her cheeks. "I love you, Maggy. Only you. Can you ever forgive me for being such an idiot?"

Laughing, she cradled his face in her hands. "I love you, too, Griffin. Now and forever."

"Will you marry me, Maggy? Spend your life with me? Have children with me?"

"Yes, I'll marry you, Griffin, and yes, I'll have your children, but you know, there are no guarantees, not in life, not in love."

He smiled, and held her tighter, letting his gaze take in her beautiful face. "I know that, Maggy, but I don't need guarantees, I've got something far more powerful."

She drew back to look up at him. "And what's that, darling?"

He laughed, then swung her off her feet again. "Trust and love, Maggy. Trust and love. Together they'll take us anywhere and everywhere we want to go. I know that now. You taught me that, and I'll never, ever forget it again." He set her down on her feet for a moment, then reached into his pocket, extracting a small, black velvet box. "I…I…hope you like it," he said nervously, handing it to her.

With shaky hands, Maggy opened the box and felt tears clog her throat. The ring was plain gold, simple and unadorned, with a square-cut diamond, sparkling with hope, with love, centered on the band. "It's beautiful." Eyes drenched, she lifted her gaze to his. "I love it. It's perfect."

"Like you, Maggy." He took the ring out of the box and slid it on her finger, ignoring the garden dirt beneath her nails. "Just like you." He bent and kissed her again. "I love you, Maggy."

"I love you, too, Griffin."

"Forever, Maggy." He hugged her tight, feeling love and warmth fill all the cold, empty places in his heart. "Forever," he whispered, knowing he was finally, truly, home.

Standing together in the morning sunlight, they kissed again, sealing their love and fulfilling their destiny.

Epilogue

Three months later...

Dear Millicent:

Hope this letter finds you and Grandpa well and enjoying your new retired life in Lake Geneva. Griffin is well and wonderful as usual, as are all my brothers. Finn took a leave of absence from the police force and is now enrolled in law school. Michael is still working undercover, so we're not sure if he'll be home for Thanksgiving or not, since no one's heard from him in a few weeks. But the rest of us will be up early Wednesday morning to spend the Thanksgiving weekend with you and Grandpa. We can't wait to see you both.

I have a question for you, though. What advice would you give to a young wife and career woman—

the only girl in a family with six boys—when she learns she's expecting…twin boys?

Love, Maggy

Dear Maggy:

My advice, dear? Blessed be! Your grandfather will be so thrilled. But I'll let you tell him yourself when we're all together at Thanksgiving. We can't wait to see you all. Drive safely. Until then…

All our love,
Millicent

* * * * *

*Be sure to look for Sharon De Vita's next
Silhouette Romance,
DADDY IN THE MAKING
featuring Michael Gallagher, in November 2004.*

Receive a FREE hardcover book from

H A R L E Q U I N   R O M A N C E®

in September!

**Harlequin Romance celebrates the launch of
the line's new cover design by offering you
this exclusive offer valid only in September,
only in Harlequin Romance.**

To receive your
FREE HARDCOVER BOOK
written by bestselling author
Emilie Richards, send us four
proofs of purchase from any
September 2004 Harlequin
Romance books. Further details
and proofs of purchase can be
found in all September 2004
Harlequin Romance books.

*Must be postmarked
no later than October 31.*

**Don't forget to be one of the first
to pick up a copy of the new-look
Harlequin Romance novels in September!**

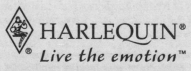

HARLEQUIN®
Live the emotion™

Visit us at www.eHarlequin.com

HRPOP0904

The *New York Times* bestselling author of
16 Lighthouse Road and *311 Pelican Court*
welcomes you back to Cedar Cove,
where life and love is anything but ordinary!

DEBBIE MACOMBER

Dear Reader,

I love living in Cedar Cove, but things just haven't been the same
since Max Russell died in our B and B. We still don't have any idea
why he came here and—most important of all—who poisoned him!

But we're not providing the only news in town. I heard that
Maryellen Sherman is getting married and her mother, Grace, has
her pick of interested men—but which one will she choose? And
Olivia Griffin is back from her honeymoon, and her mother, Charlotte,
has a man in her life, too, but I'm not sure Olivia's too pleased....

There's plenty of other gossip I could tell you. Come by for a cup
of tea and one of my blueberry muffins and we'll talk.

44
*Cranberry
Point*

"**Macomber is known for her honest portrayals of
ordinary women in small-town America, and this tale
cements her position as an icon of the genre.**"
—*Publishers Weekly* on *16 Lighthouse Road*

*Available the first week of September 2004,
wherever paperbacks are sold.*

COMING NEXT MONTH

#1738 THEIR LITTLE COWGIRL—Myrna Mackenzie
In a Fairy Tale World...
How can plain-Jane Jackie Hammond be the biological mother
of sexy rancher Stephen Collins's adorable daughter when
she's never even met him? Ask the fertility clinic! But before
Jackie gives up her newfound child, she might discover that her
little girl—and the one man who makes Jackie feel beautiful—
are worth fighting for.

#1739 GEORGIA GETS HER GROOM!—Carolyn Zane
The Brubaker Brides
Georgia Brubaker has her sights set on the perfect man.
But when she comes face-to-face with her childhood nemesis,
all her plans go out the window. The nerdy "Cootie Biggles"
has developed into supersmooth, 007-clone Carter Biggles-
Vanderhousen, who leaves Georgia shaken *and* stirred....

#1740 THE BILLIONAIRE'S WEDDING MASQUER-
ADE—Melissa McClone
Billionaires don't make very good farmhands! But
Elisabeth Wheeler is desperate for help, and Henry Davenport
is strong, available...and handsome. Henry might not have any
experience planting or ploughing, but he sure knows how to
make Elisabeth's pulse race!

#1741 CINDERELLA'S LUCKY TICKET—
Melissa James
When Lucy Miles tries to claim the house Ben Capriati won
in a sweepstakes drawing, he knows he should be furious. But
he just can't fight his attraction to the sweet but sassy librarian.
Can Ben convince Lucy to build a home with him forever?

SRCNM0904